"The funniest, quirkiest romance of the year." Marie Phillips

"Genius. Buy it, borrow it, steal it but just make sure you read it. I am willing to bet it will be your surprise read of the year. I read it on the train home the day I received it and spent the whole evening smiling." Scott Pack, meandmybigmouth Blog

"An adorable book: neat, sweet, petite. Your loved one will love you even more for buying it for them." Toby Litt

"One of the saddest, funniest, strangest, and most romantic books ... Brilliant!" *The Bookseller*

"Simply brilliant. A real gem of a book ... this ode to love was built to last." *Ham & High*

"... may technically be called a love story, but if it is, it is one that is blissfully cliché free. More please." Pulp.net

"Somebody should write Mr Kaufman and thank him for his tender heart. I expect this story will replace boxes of chocolates and flowers in courting rituals to come." Sheila Heti

"This story will steal up quietly and seduce with its originality and wit." Terry Griggs

Andrew Kaufman

THE WATERPROOF BIBLE

TELEGRAM

This first edition published in 2010 by Telegram

ISBN: 978-1-84659-086-3

A full CIP record for this book is available from the British Library.
A full CIP record for this book is available from the Library of Congress.

Printed in the UK by CPI Cox & Wyman, Reading, Berks, RG1 8EX

TELEGRAM
26 Westbourne Grove, London W2 5RH, UK
2398 Doswell Avenue, Saint Paul, Minnesota, 55108, US
Verdun, Beirut, Lebanon
www.telegrambooks.com

For Marlo

PART ONE

Keepsakes

Rebecca 1

1

The woman who couldn't keep her feelings to herself

The limousine taking Rebecca Reynolds and Lewis Taylor to the funeral had stalled in the middle of an intersection. The long black car faced west on Queen, straddling Broadview Avenue in the east end of Toronto, Ontario, Canada. Rebecca and Lewis sat on opposite ends of the bench seat, and no one sat between them.

Although they were both grieving the loss of Lisa Taylor—Rebecca's little sister and Lewis's wife—the two were similar in few other ways. Lewis was relatively short. Both his suit and his haircut were fashionable. Rebecca was quite tall, her naturally brown hair cut in a shoulder-length bob, and she wore a simple black dress. But as the driver repeatedly turned the key in the ignition, they each stared out their own window, mirroring each other.

Rebecca idly wondered if it was a problem with the engine or whether they'd simply run out of gas. She ran her hands over her skirt until the fabric was without wrinkles. She realized that this corner was close to E.Z. Self Storage, where she rented unit #207. She played with her clutch, snapping the clasp open and closed. Then she looked down at the carpeted floor and remembered that she was in a limousine, travelling to her sister's funeral. Her grief, sadness and guilt returned.

As Rebecca felt these emotions, Lewis became overwhelmed with them as well. The grief, sadness and guilt were heavy and painful. It had been three days and eleven hours since he'd discovered his wife's body, but until now Lewis had felt nothing. A sense of relief flooded through him. Then he remembered that he was sitting beside Rebecca and that these feelings weren't his own, but hers.

"Oh," Lewis said.

"Yeah," Rebecca replied.

"Yeah," Lewis repeated. The grief radiating from his sister-in-law only made Lewis more aware of his failure and Rebecca's overwhelming ability to push her emotions into the world as surely as her lungs pushed out her breath.

Rebecca had been able to project her emotions since the day she was born, when everything was dark and then suddenly it was bright and there were colours. Rebecca didn't know where she was going. She hadn't known there was somewhere to go. It hurt and there was no way to resist. She couldn't focus her eyes, didn't know she had eyes, and didn't know that the light and the colours were coming through them.

When hands first touched her, Rebecca didn't know

what hands were, what skin was, what touch was. Only that the thub-thub was missing. There had been darkness and the thub-thub, and they'd been consistent and soothing, but now both were missing. The newborn Rebecca became quite distressed. Feelings of great anxiety and fear went through her and they did not stop there. They went into the room. They went inside everyone. The doctor stopped and stared at the baby in his hands. The nurses turned from the stainless steel tray and stared helplessly at each other. The hum of the machines became audible.

"What's wrong with her? What's wrong?" Rebecca's mother asked.

The doctor didn't know what was wrong, so he did what he normally did. Cutting the cord, he laid the baby across her mother's chest. Rebecca heard the thub-thub. She closed her eyes and the darkness was back. She began to feel calm and safe, and she broadcast these feelings to everyone in the room. The doctor and nurses sighed. The mother put her hands on top of the baby. The delivery room became still and quiet, and Rebecca fell asleep.

Not every one of Rebecca's feelings travelled the same distance—the more intense her emotion, the farther it went. To feel her happiness at finding her favourite show on TV you'd have to be very close to her head, almost touching it. But when she fell in love, people a full city block away knew. This caused many problems, since the things Rebecca wanted most to keep to herself were the ones she broadcast the farthest.

The limousine was still stalled in the middle of the intersection when Rebecca looked out her window and noticed a white Honda Civic rapidly approaching. It did not slow down.

"That car is going to hit us," she said, quietly.

Having felt Rebecca's anxiety, Lewis had already turned his head. When the white Honda Civic was less than half a block away and still showed no signs of stopping, Lewis and Rebecca noticed something extraordinarily peculiar.

"Do you see that?" Lewis asked.

"Yes," Rebecca replied.

The driver of the Honda Civic seemed to have green skin. Just as they noticed this, the creature finally hit the brakes. The back wheels locked, the tires squealed, the smell of burnt rubber was pungent, but the white Honda Civic kept skidding towards the limousine. With only inches remaining between its front bumper and the back door of the limousine on Rebecca's side, the car finally stopped. For ten seconds the occupants of both vehicles sat motionless, staring at each other through the two planes of glass separating them. Lewis and Rebecca were so focused on the green-skinned woman that neither heard the driver restart the engine. The limo lurched forward, pushing them back against their seats. Another sudden stop a moment later threw them to the floor.

Rebecca's face was pressed against the carpet, which smelled of both bleach and champagne. Scrambling, she got out of the limousine. She was so intent on catching another glimpse of the white Honda Civic's driver that she didn't stoop to pick up the contents of her purse, which had spilled onto the road. Rebecca exited the limo and Lewis soon joined her, as did the limo driver. The three of them stood in the middle of the intersection. Rebecca noticed that the car had Nova Scotia plates as it travelled south on Broadview, picked up speed and took the first left without signalling.

"That was close," the driver said. Rebecca nodded in agreement. Lewis raised his hands and began backing away. He'd been confident that the grief he so desperately wanted to feel would soon arrive. But now, having nearly been killed by a woman with green skin, it was easy to believe that stranger things could happen and that his grieving might never begin. Keeping his hands raised and ignoring the honking of the cars whose path he blocked, Lewis continued to back away from the limousine.

"Lewis? Where are you going?" Rebecca asked, projecting her confusion across two lanes of traffic.

"I can't go to the funeral."

"Why not?"

"Because she'll be there. She'll see me. She'll know."

"Know what?"

"I'm so sorry."

Gesturing with his right hand, Lewis hailed a taxi, which stopped in front of him. "You'll regret this," Rebecca shouted. Her anger reached pedestrians on the far side of the street, causing some to stop and stare, while others scurried away. Lewis climbed inside the cab and shut the door. He looked straight ahead but continued to feel Rebecca's anger as clearly as if it were his own.

2

The many reasons why
Rebecca Reynolds hates Lewis Taylor

As the limousine finally cleared the intersection of Queen and Broadview, Rebecca kicked off her shoes, lay on her back, pressed the bottoms of her feet against the cold glass of the passenger window and began making a list of the reasons she hated Lewis Taylor. These came easily to her. *One: he's arrogant. Two: he's an asshole. Three: he'll never, ever, understand how irreplaceable she is.* She was at number twelve before the limo reached Parliament Street, and the list kept growing as they continued driving west on Queen.

Keeping her feet against the glass, Rebecca closed her eyes. She took deep breaths, knowing that her anger would upset the driver. She kept still but could not calm down. Raising her arm, Rebecca checked her watch, seeing that she had thirty minutes to get to the church. She sat up and lowered the tinted window between her and the driver. "Please don't get there until just before 1:30," she said. She raised the partition and lay back down on the bench seat of the limousine. As she felt the car make a sharp right, Rebecca tried to pinpoint the exact moment she had begun hating Lewis Taylor and realized it was the first time she'd met him.

Rebecca had come home from university for an unannounced visit. It was mid-afternoon and, as she'd expected, the house was empty. Lisa was still in high school and her parents were both at work. She made a sandwich and went to her former bedroom to study. Several hours later, she was still trying to memorize the atomic weights of the elements when she heard loud music. Shutting her textbook, Rebecca went downstairs. The music got louder, but she was in the living room before she understood that it was being performed live, in the basement. Midway down the basement stairs, Rebecca saw that Lisa was playing a keyboard, while a drum machine ticked and a boy Rebecca did not recognize sang into a microphone. Lisa was in a rock band, or, more accurately, a synth-pop duo. The boy's voice was terrible—thin and whiny. His haircut was trendy and his posture calculatedly slouchy. By the time she reached the bottom step, Rebecca had already projected her dislike of him into the room.

Lisa and Lewis were startled not so much by Rebecca's unannounced appearance as by the dislike that radiated from her. Lewis turned off his microphone, setting it on the floor. Lisa kept her fingers on the keys, her synthesizer producing a long, sustained E chord.

As she stood there, Rebecca found one more reason to dislike Lewis: he was oblivious to the fact that Lisa was in love with him, a reality Rebecca recognized by the way her sister's hips were angled towards him and how she kept looking at him, using only her eyes to smile.

"Um, this is my sister," Lisa finally said, taking her hands off the keys. The drum machine continued to tick. "Rebecca, this is Lewis."

"Good to meet you, Rebecca."

Rebecca did not reply with words.

"Maybe we should call it a day?" Lisa asked.

Lewis had already grabbed his bag. "Later," he said, watching his feet.

The driver opened her door before Rebecca noticed that the limo had stopped. She looked at her watch: 1:35. She put her shoes back on, ending her list with the most powerful reason to hate Lewis Taylor: he had failed to keep her sister safe.

Inside the church, Rebecca saw her mother in the foyer, surrounded by two uncles and an aunt. Rebecca hovered at the edge of this group, with her hands clasped firmly behind her back. Desperately wanting to smoke, she opened her purse to find her nicotine gum—a temporary measure she'd been using for two years. She looked inside, easily found the package and began pushing a piece out of the plastic wrapping. The crinkling seemed out of place, echoing through the church foyer, but she didn't stop. Not even when both of her uncles turned their bald heads in her direction.

Rebecca noticed that her mother's slip was showing, pushed past the crowd and took her mother's hand. She wanted to offer support, not receive it, but when her mother felt Rebecca's worry, she tightened her grip, making her daughter feel safe.

Shortly after her seventh birthday, Rebecca stood on her neighbour's lawn and held Lisa's hand as they watched an attendant push their mother up the front walk. It was the first time they had seen her in seven months. Her mother bounced when the wheelchair hit a crack in the sidewalk. Her arms rested on top of an orange blanket, and her skin was very pale. Rebecca wanted to wave, but she was afraid her mother wouldn't wave back. The attendants carried her mother up the steps and through the door that her father held open.

"There she is," Rebecca told Lisa.

She led Lisa to the backyard and the two girls sat facing the house, looking up to the second-floor window where they knew their mother was now sleeping. Lisa pulled up a fist full of grass. She threw it back on the ground. She looked up at Rebecca.

"I'm scared, too," Lisa said.

"They wouldn't let her come home if she wasn't better," Rebecca said. She tried to think about anything else, but couldn't.

"Why won't they let us see her?"

"She's tired. We can see her tomorrow," Rebecca said.

At six o'clock Rebecca and Lisa were allowed back into the house. Dinner was in the microwave. Her father was making phone calls. Rebecca turned on the TV and found her sister's favourite show. She raised the volume louder than it had ever been before. When her father did not ask her to turn it down, Rebecca took off her shoes and snuck through the kitchen. She climbed the stairs on her tiptoes. She was a little out of breath when she reached the top and stood in front of the door to the guest room. The door was old and didn't shut tight. Rebecca looked through the gap. She saw her mother lying on her side, facing away. Rebecca pushed the door with her index finger until it was halfway open, and then she went into the room, moving as quietly as she could.

The blinds were down, so the room was dark, but some late-afternoon sunlight snuck through the gap between the shade and the windowsill. Her mother continued to sleep. Her blankets had slid down. She was wearing a hospital gown that tied at the back. Her skin was very white and her hair was too long. Rebecca walked to the side of the bed but did not reach out to touch her.

"It's okay, baby," Rebecca's mother said. Although her eyes remained closed, she'd heard her daughter's distress. "I'm not too far. No? Right here."

Rebecca touched her mom's arm. Her skin was damp and cool. Her mother rolled onto her back, and Rebecca knew she couldn't stay. Nothing in the room felt like it was supposed to: the light coming from the edge of the blinds; the colour of her mother's clothes; the smell of medications coming from the bedside table—all of it was wrong. Rebecca had to leave the room, but she needed something to take with her. An object she could hold, something that would continually confirm that her mother had come home. She knew she couldn't take the pill bottles, because their absence would be noticed. She looked around, but there were very few things in the room that hadn't been there before her mother's return. Then she saw the identification bracelet that her mother had been wearing when they'd carried her into the house.

The bracelet had been cut and lay on the nightstand, but her mother's full name was clearly visible in purple type. Rebecca reached for it, and when her fist was tight, she felt something very strange. The sensation was almost electric and pushed out from her chest into her arm, through her fingertips and into the broken plastic bracelet. It made her feel like she needed to pee, and then it disappeared completely. Rebecca opened her fist and looked at the bracelet, but nothing on the outside had changed. Keeping the bracelet tightly in her hand, Rebecca left the room, closing the door as much as she could.

Putting most of her weight on the banister so that she could move as soundlessly as possible, Rebecca was attempting to sneak down the stairs when she met her father on the second landing. She closed her fist tightly to make sure the plastic bracelet could not be seen. Her father looked over her head to the door of the guest room, then back at Rebecca.

"Did you see her?"

"Yes."

"Are you okay?"

"Yes," Rebecca said. This was a lie. Everything about seeing her mother weak, tired and vulnerable had disturbed Rebecca. As these feelings went through her, she waited for her father to hear them, but he didn't. Her father simply smiled.

"That's great. We should have let you see her earlier. I'm sorry." He hugged her, then turned and walked down the stairs. Once her father was completely out of sight, she opened her hand and stared at the bracelet, knowing it was the only thing that was different.

For the next six weeks, while Rebecca's mother remained in bed, Rebecca carried the plastic bracelet with her at all times. She held it in her hand while she slept. She kept it in the front right pocket of whichever pair of pants she was wearing. She never forgot to bring it with her, not even once. When someone asked her how her she was doing, Rebecca could just say fine and they would believe her. Rebecca Reynolds finally had the power to lie.

Seven weeks later, Rebecca came home from school and found her mother watching television in the living room. She wore her housecoat, and her skin was still pale, but this was the first time Rebecca had seen her outside of the guest room.

"Come here, baby," her mother said.

Rebecca climbed onto the couch, curling up beside her. Together they watched The Edge of Night. Things felt normal and Rebecca knew that this moment would have been impossible if the bracelet hadn't been in her pocket. Otherwise, she would have been too afraid to let her mother feel how frightened she really was.

After the success of the bracelet, other experiments quickly followed. When she failed to land an axel in competition, Rebecca kept her skate laces. When her teacher gave her a failing grade, she took his coffee mug. When Jenny Benders didn't invite her to her birthday party, she stole her hair clip.

All of her keepsakes were put into a shoebox, which she kept underneath her bed. It wasn't long before there were two shoeboxes. Then three and four and five.

When Rebecca turned fourteen, she began collecting mementos from all the good moments in her life. Her emotions had become so powerful and important to her that when one of them left her, she felt incredibly vulnerable. Keeping these feelings of joy to herself kept her from feeling exposed. It gave her some privacy. It soon became a habit that every time Rebecca experienced a moment that produced any significant emotion, happy or sad, she stored a souvenir.

The number of boxes under her bed grew and grew. By the time she was sixteen, the shoeboxes were stacked three high and took up all the space under her bed. When she went to university, she took the shoeboxes with her and rented apartments based on closet space. When the closets weren't big enough, she got rid of her roommate and used the second bedroom. Then the living room. Then the kitchen. Finally, Rebecca rented unit #207 from E.Z. Self Storage near the corner of Queen and Broadview in downtown Toronto and moved all of her boxes there, where they were safely secured under lock and key.

"Where's Dad?" Rebecca asked.

"He's inside. Where's Lewis?"

Rebecca's response was a guilty feeling, mystifying her mother. She felt guilty because it was her fault that Lisa had married Lewis in the first place.

When Lisa finished high school, she and Lewis had moved to Halifax together to attend the Nova Scotia College of Art and Design. Lewis still thought of Lisa as nothing more than a friend—the apartment they rented had two bedrooms. Even more than she hated Lewis, Rebecca hated knowing that her sister would never get her heart's desire.

Both sisters were home from university for the holiday, and on Christmas Eve their mother sent them to buy wrapping paper. It was a task easily accomplished. With time to kill and a desire to avoid a relative-filled house, Rebecca and Lisa drove around and eventually parked in the lot of their old high school.

"Do you remember those white jeans that Phillip Wilson used to wear?" Rebecca asked.

"Lewis still thinks of me as a friend. I don't know what to do."

For some moments it was quiet inside the car. For once, it was Rebecca who saw the simple solution. "Where are the bedrooms in your apartment?" she asked.

"At the front."

"Right next to each other?"

"Yes."

"So you share a wall?"

"Yeah."

"How thick is it?"

"It's not thick at all." Lisa turned in her seat and faced

her sister. "It's really thin. Are you suggesting what I think you are?"

"Do you really love him?"

"You know I do."

"Is he worthy of you?"

"I know you don't think he is, but he really is."

"So, yes, I am suggesting that. Everyone and anyone. Start the night you get back, if you can."

Lisa took her older sister's advice. The shared wall proved even less soundproof than imagined. Lewis lasted three weeks. Nineteen months later, they were married. Rebecca's plan had worked, and she'd never forgiven herself for it.

"Rebecca?" her mother repeated.

"We almost got in an accident. Then he just left. He walked away. He said he was sorry." Rebecca looked up at her mother and tried to smile. "Should we go in?"

"Okay."

Still holding her mother's hand as they walked into the church, Rebecca saw her father sitting in a pew at the very front. But as they walked towards him, Rebecca began to feel very strange. With each step she took the strange feeling grew. And as she took her seat beside her father, she realized it wasn't a strange feeling. It was no feeling at all.

3

Forty-five square feet of canvas

One thousand, eight hundred and four kilometres west of Lisa's funeral, Stewart Findley waited on the top step of the only post office in Morris, Manitoba. Metaphorically, Stewart was waiting for a number of things to happen, but at this precise moment he was waiting for Margaret, his boss, who was now forty-seven minutes late.

Taking his cellphone from his pocket, Stewart confirmed that he had no missed calls and then hopped down the steps to the sidewalk. He looked south down Main Street but still didn't see her. He kicked the large cube, which was made of several layers of folded canvas, at the bottom of the stairs, then turned and continued to wait. As he checked his cellphone again, he heard Margaret's truck.

The truck came into view, red, old and given to as many eccentricities as its driver. Seeing Margaret behind the wheel, Stewart tried once again to guess her age. Of all the strange things about her—she seldom blinked, her skin often had a greenish tinge to it, she was very strong, and she owned and operated a hotel that rarely had guests—it was her indeterminate age that Stewart found the most perplexing. He had been the Prairie Embassy Hotel's only employee for three and a half years, but he had never been able to figure out how old Margaret was. His highest guess was seventy and his lowest was thirty-seven; with both estimations he'd been confident that he'd finally got it right. As Stewart watched Margaret park in front of the post office, he made another guess: fifty-seven, as there was something taxed and sweaty about her today.

Leaving the engine running, Margaret slid across the seat and out the passenger door. She kissed Stewart on both cheeks. "The goddamn council meeting went long," she said. "Guess what the idiot's solution to the drought is?"

"Which idiot is this?"

"The mayor. Fifty-four days, with crops perishing in the fields, and what's his brilliant idea? He's hiring rainmakers. Two of them, father and son. I said they could stay at the hotel for free."

Stewart ordinarily had little interest in the doings of the Morris Town Council, and today he cared even less. With a sweeping motion, he pointed to the cube of folded canvas on the sidewalk. It measured three feet on each side. Margaret immediately recognized what it was.

"Is that it?" she asked.

"It is."

"Your boat has a sail!" Margaret punched him in the arm, the impact knocking Stewart off balance.

For three years, six months and one day Stewart had been the Prairie Embassy Hotel's only employee. This, less three weeks, was exactly the amount of time he'd been building his sailboat. Although Margaret had witnessed every stage of construction, she'd never commented on the fact that he was building a sailboat in the middle of the Canadian Prairies. Or, more specifically, on a bend of the Red River that could float a boat only once a year, for a few days during spring runoff. But Margaret was not someone who needed to pry. This was partly her respect for privacy and partly due to her love of eccentricity, but mainly because she had secrets of her own.

Stewart opened the tailgate. Margaret adjusted her scarf and they each picked up a side of the sail.

"It's heavy," she said.

Stewart nodded his agreement, rendered speechless by the weight. Taking tiny steps, they moved towards the back of the truck.

"One, two, three," Margaret said. On three they heaved it into the bed. The truck rocked on its springs, and a thin layer of dirt was knocked to the ground. Stewart closed the tailgate.

"Should we tie it down?" Margaret asked.

"It's not going anywhere," Stewart said, but he drove slowly. They had made it past the town's population sign when his cellphone rang. Stewart looked down at his phone. Margaret studied his face.

"It's her. I can tell," she said.

"What if it is?"

"Then you just don't answer it," Margaret said, trying to pull the phone out of his hand.

"She's just lost her sister!" Stewart said, holding the ringing phone as far away from Margaret as possible.

"That's true," Margaret said. Her hands fell to her lap. "You're right. I'm sorry. Answer it, then."

Stewart nodded. He swerved onto the shoulder and stopped.

"Rebecca?" he said to his wife, a woman he had not seen in three years, six months and one day.

～

Stewart had met his wife not by accident but because of one. Pushing an overly burdened grocery cart across an icy parking lot, he'd slipped. The cart got away from him and rolled towards a row of parked cars, picking up speed on the ice. Lying prone, he predicted that it would hit either the rusted Ford Tempo or the cherry red Karmann Ghia.

To his surprise, Stewart hoped it would be the Karmann Ghia, although he wasn't sure why. If it hit the Tempo, the bumper would absorb the impact, whereas a collision with the Karmann Ghia would destroy the right tail light. Stewart watched as the cart, seemingly of its own will, veered slightly left and struck the Karmann Ghia. As predicted, it shattered the tail light.

Stewart got up and retrieved his cart. He was squatting to survey the damage when a shadow crossed his face. Looking up, he found Rebecca looking down.

"Had a bit of an accident," he said, words he would later conclude to be the worst opening line in the history of love.

"I can see that."

"I can fix it." He raised his head and looked her in the eye. Somehow he could feel her doubt. Not just by inferring, or assuming, or being empathetic—he literally felt it. "Honest, I'm good with my hands," Stewart said and, as if to demonstrate, he produced a business card.

"General Repairs," she said, studying his card. "Impressive."

Her voice was icy, but Stewart knew—again, he could feel—that she was actually quite attracted to him. He had always had trouble reading women, but this one seemed unable to hide her true feelings, which made her very appealing. Plus, she had long, shapely legs that even in the dead of winter were covered not by pants, a long skirt or a parka, but just by black tights and shapely boots.

"I'll need your phone number," Stewart said. He realized that she was only feigning impatience as she asked for another card and wrote down her contact information on the back.

The replacement tail light was more expensive than he'd hoped, but three days later Stewart phoned ahead and went to her house, tools in hand. Finding the car parked on the street, Stewart began work and was crouched beside the rear bumper when he felt her shadow on him.

"Good morning," Stewart said.

"Hello. Make sure you do it right."

"I will."

"Just remember, I don't trust you at all," she said. Stewart felt that the opposite was true.

He did not question being able to feel this woman's emotions. Stewart rarely thought anything was strange. This was one of his gifts. Another was his innate ability to build or fix anything. It was as if he could hear how the pieces wanted to fit together. They were not exactly speaking to him, not with words, but they let him know what needed to be done. The proof was irrefutable in the cars he'd rebuilt, the houses he'd rewired and the lifespan of household appliances he'd greatly extended, so Stewart just didn't question it.

He'd finished the job before his hands were cold. Rebecca had stayed with him, watching over his shoulder.

"Do you want to pop the hood?" he asked her.

"Why?"

"I just thought I'd give it a look over."

"The engine's in the trunk."

"Right."

He looked at Rebecca. Her arms were crossed in front of her chest, and her face held a sour expression—yet he could feel how much she liked him. With this in mind, he opened the trunk, bent over the motor and over-tightened the butterfly valve, ensuring that the car would have problems as soon as the temperature dropped below -10° C.

"Listen, if you have any more problems, just call me," he said.

"I have your card."

"Don't hesitate to call."

Three weeks later, there was a cold snap. But it wasn't until he'd rescued her for the third time that Stewart finally found the courage to ask her out.

"Rebecca? Why aren't you at the funeral?"

"I am. Stewart, listen to me. Something horrible has happened. I've lost my love for Lisa."

"What?"

"Or at least, I'm losing it. It's not all gone. But some of it is."

"You've lost what?"

"You're not listening!"

Stewart felt how scared she was. One of the strangest things, of the many strange things, about his relationship with Rebecca was that Stewart could feel her emotions through the telephone. This did not happen when Rebecca talked on the phone with anyone else. Stewart was the only one.

"I'm sorry, Rebecca, I'm just not getting it. What's happened?"

"It's all about when she moved out . . ."

"That's the story you're telling at the funeral?"

"Yes, but just listen. I can remember everything about it. All the facts. The rain. What the van looked like. What Lisa was wearing. That's not the problem."

"What is it?"

"Just listen. Please. The problem is that it doesn't make me feel anything. Not happy, or sad, or how I loved her more than ever when she came back. All those emotions are gone. They've vanished. They're just gone!"

"That's, that's . . ." Stewart said. "Hold on for a second."

Making a worried face to Margaret, Stewart got out of the truck and walked into the wheat field he'd parked beside. The stalks grew higher the deeper into the field he went. He continued walking. The stalks were slightly taller than his waist, but he still didn't know what to say.

4

The Derrick Miller memory

Rebecca sat on a child-sized chair in the basement of the church. Having hastily excused herself to go to the washroom, Rebecca had come down here instead. She assumed that someone was already looking for her, and knew that it wouldn't be long before they'd find her. She had not turned on the overhead fluorescents, leaving the glow of her cellphone as her only source of light. Feeling disproportionately gigantic, she moved her phone from her right hand to her left, pressing it firmly against her ear as she eagerly waited to hear her estranged husband's advice.

"For the time being, let's forget about why it's happened," Stewart finally said. "It's just happened. You know? Who knows why? These things just happen. Okay?"

This perspective was precisely what she needed to hear. The fact that Stewart never questioned the strange things that commonly happened to Rebecca was the main reason that she'd fallen in love with him. It was certainly why she loved him still. Stewart never doubted her, or made her feel weird. He just listened, then immediately began constructing a way for her to cope.

"So, are all your memories affected?" he asked.

"No. Just that one. Well, no others that I know of."

"But it's the one you're using for the eulogy?"

"Yes," Rebecca said.

"Why can't you use it?"

"Because it doesn't make me feel anything. I'd feel false and phoney, and people would feel it."

"So just use another one, then. You've got tons of them."

"But that was the perfect one."

"What about the party?"

"What party?"

"The one that went wrong. The Derrick Miller party."

"I don't think . . ."

"Try it. I'll wait."

"Okay," Rebecca said.

Setting her phone in her lap, she leaned forward and looked at her shiny black shoes. She closed her eyes. She saw her fifteen-year-old face reflected in the front hall mirror of her parents' house. Her parents had gone away for the weekend, leaving Rebecca and Lisa alone, which was something that had never happened before. In her right hand was a telephone and on the other end of the line was Derrick Miller.

"I'm thinking of maybe having a party," Rebecca said, studying her pores in the mirror.

"When?" Derrick asked.

"Tonight."

"Do it!"

"I don't know, though."

"No, do it. Completely."

"You think?"

"Definitely."

"Who should I invite?"

"Everybody!"

"You think?" Rebecca asked. This was more ambitious than her original plan.

"For sure!" Derrick said.

"All right. I'm doing it."

Rebecca began making calls. Derrick Miller made many more. The first guests arrived at 7:30 p.m., and although Rebecca recognized their faces, she didn't know their names. They entered her home without taking off their shoes. They opened the refrigerator and moved condiments to the kitchen floor to make room for beer. Sitting on the kitchen counter, they talked amongst themselves. Bottles were opened, caps fell to the linoleum, and Rebecca attempted to laugh in all the right places.

By 9:00 p.m. the party was already a success. Teenagers stood shoulder to shoulder in the kitchen. Music Rebecca had never heard before played on her family's stereo. No one was using coasters. With a roll of paper towels under her arm, Rebecca travelled from room to room, sopping up spills. The first glass was broken just before ten. Around eleven a painting was knocked off the wall in the living room. Just after midnight people started smoking in the house and a couple disappeared upstairs.

At 1:00 a.m. Rebecca noticed a bottle of peach schnapps on the kitchen counter. Her arms full of empties, she stopped. Derrick Miller was down on all fours, his head completely inside the liquor cabinet.

"What are you doing?" Rebecca asked, her voice high and squeaky.

The beer bottles in her left hand were slipping. Derrick pulled his head out of the liquor cabinet.

"Just don't," Rebecca said. Putting her index finger in her mouth, Rebecca began biting her fingernails. She was filled with anxiety. She felt like the party was now beyond her control. These feelings went into the heads of everyone in the kitchen. They went into the head of Derrick Miller, who reached into the liquor cabinet, pulled out a bottle of vodka, then released a short, disdainful laugh. Derrick twisted off the lid. The cap fell to the linoleum and spun. Derrick raised the bottle and saluted her. Lifting it to his mouth, he drank. The guests in the kitchen cheered, and Rebecca's anxiety increased.

The more distress she felt, the more emboldened her houseguests became. She began biting her right thumbnail as they began laughing louder. Derrick Miller coughed, wiped his mouth with the back of his sleeve and passed the vodka to his right. The partiers cheered. The bottle was passed through the hands of three people, and then it stopped. All laughter ceased. Derrick looked to his right and up. Following his eyes, Rebecca discovered her little sister standing in the doorway of the kitchen.

Twelve-year-old Lisa was supposed to be attending a sleepover at Ruth Montgomery's house. She'd thought it was going to be just her and Ruth, but when she arrived six other girls were there. Suspecting that the worst aspects of prepubescent girls were about to be displayed, Lisa endured the gossip about older boys and girls not in attendance. But minutes after midnight, fuelled by sugar, overtiredness and the need for approval, the other girls started ganging up on Lisa. They teased her because her nightgown was made of flannel and her hair was messy, whereas theirs looked like it had been ironed. They excluded her, forming a clique in the process, and Lisa suspected that this was the reason she'd been invited in the first place.

Lisa had really wanted to be friends with Ruth, but she'd found Ruth's friends boring and stupid. Her feelings were hurt but not broken. While they were busy trying to catch glimpses of a scrambled movie on upper cable, Lisa changed into her clothes, packed her things and walked home. Leaving felt like victory, but when she arrived, Lisa was surprised to find her house filled with teenagers. Standing in the doorway between the living room and the kitchen, she pointed her index finger directly at Derrick Miller, a boy she knew to be no good.

"What are you doing in my house?" she said and then, taking a step into the kitchen, she saw her sister. Rebecca looked at the kitchen floor, and Lisa instantly felt her shame. Without looking at anyone in the room, Lisa walked through the kitchen.

Rebecca listened to the basement door open and close.

She heard Lisa walk down the steps. The guests laughed. Derrick Miller continued laughing after everyone else had stopped. As the bottle of vodka was passed back to him, every light in the house went out, the stereo slurring to a stop.

Rebecca stepped back, leaned against the wall of the kitchen and held the beer bottles tightly against her chest. She tried to make herself small. She wanted to become invisible. She concentrated on thinking nothing at all.

"What happened?" someone said.

"I don't know."

"Lame."

The refrigerator door opened and bottles clinked in the darkness. The kitchen cleared. The front door opened. In five minutes the house was empty and silent. Rebecca heard a click from the basement. The lights came back on. The record player started playing. She couldn't believe how loud it was. She set the beer bottles on the kitchen table. Picking up the vodka bottle, Rebecca peeled off the label and put it in her pocket, then she went into the living room and turned off the stereo. When Rebecca returned, Lisa was at the kitchen table with an empty beer case in her hand.

Lisa started collecting bottles. Rebecca joined her. Lisa still wouldn't look up. Rebecca gathered beer caps and coffee mugs that had served as ashtrays. She swept up broken glass. They opened every window in the house and filled an orange plastic bucket with soap and water. The stains on the carpet, the coffee table in the living room and the linoleum in the kitchen were all scrubbed. They rehung the painting that had been knocked to the floor. They washed the sheets from the master bedroom. They remade the bed. They did all this work without saying a word or making eye contact.

When they were finished, it was four in the morning. They stood shoulder to shoulder at the bottom of the stairs, Rebecca staring at the carpet. Reaching up, Lisa grabbed her older sister's chin. Rebecca was shocked by her sister's aggressive gesture as Lisa's fingernails dug into her cheeks.

"You know, you don't have to make them like you," Lisa said.

Rebecca did not know what to say. She had expected to be extorted by her little sister, or at least made fun of. Biting her bottom lip, Rebecca shrugged agreement.

"Just promise me you won't do anything this stupid again."

Rebecca didn't say a word, but her cheeks grew red and shame radiated from her every pore.

"Okay," Lisa said. She held Rebecca's face for a second longer, then let go and went to bed. She never told.

Rebecca opened her eyes and looked at the dingy linoleum floor of the church basement.

"Rebecca? Rebecca?" she heard. She turned her head and was momentarily surprised when she did not see Stewart beside her. Looking down, she saw the cellphone, which explained why his voice seemed so tiny and far away.

"I'm here."

"And?"

"Yeah, that one's going to work," Rebecca said. The Derrick Miller memory made her feel tremendous love and respect for Lisa. It reminded her how much joy she felt simply to have known her, let alone been her older sister.

"There you go."

"Thanks, Stewart."

"You're gonna do great."

"Plus, I think I lost my keys."

"Don't worry about that right now. You have a second set."

"I even have a third."

"You're going to be fine."

"Thanks, Stewart."

"Okay, then. Call me after?"

"I will."

"Okay," Stewart said, but Rebecca hung up her phone before he finished, as she didn't want him to feel how much she missed him.

Going upstairs, Rebecca met a bald uncle coming down.

"Where were you?"

"I got lost."

"We've been waiting."

"Let's go," she said.

Rebecca walked to the front pew, where she sat between her mother and father. She opened a hymn book. She looked down and noticed an ant crawling along the worn hardwood floor. Watching its progress,

Rebecca lost track of time until she felt an elbow push into her ribs. Turning to her right, she saw her mother smiling sadly.

"It's you now."

"Oh," Rebecca said. She looked up. From behind the pulpit, Reverend Stevenson stared over his glasses at her, his left eyebrow weirdly magnified by the lens. She stood. The hymn book fell to the floor. The sound echoed through the church. Rebecca bent over and reached for the book, but it slipped from her fingers, falling to the floor a second time.

"Go, just go," her mother whispered.

Leaving the book on the floor, Rebecca pushed past shifted knees into the aisle. She walked to the casket. She looked down. She stayed like this, looking, until the minister cleared his throat. Startled, Rebecca turned and then walked behind the pulpit. She folded her hands behind her back. She let them fall to her sides. She took a very deep breath, but as she opened her mouth to speak, Rebecca realized that all of her emotions surrounding the Derrick Miller memory had disappeared. The facts remained clear—she could see the teenage girls in tight jeans, Derrick Miller's long black hair and the vodka bottle on the kitchen floor. But all the emotions had seemingly evaporated. The joy, love and respect she'd felt not twenty minutes earlier were gone.

The church remained silent. Rebecca looked at her hands. She searched for another memory. She remembered several: when Lisa had refused to move into her new bedroom; when she'd gotten into trouble at summer camp; when she'd driven the car at fourteen. But there were no emotions connected to these memories, either. Their absence caused Rebecca to feel a number of different things: surprise, anxiety and even fear. But what she felt most was shame. Two days after Lisa's death, her love had already weakened.

This shame left Rebecca. It went to everyone sitting in the church. Women felt the shame that radiated from Rebecca and wondered what could possibly have caused it. Men looked up from the floor, anger visible in the corners of their eyes. There was no sound. No one moved. Neither her mother nor her father would look up from the floor as Rebecca stepped from the pulpit. Keeping her head down, she walked to the back of the church and through the doorway, the large wooden doors closing behind her.

PART TWO

One Great City

Lewis 1

5

The first haircut of the rest of his life

Twenty-six hours after his wife's funeral ended, Lewis Taylor looked through the peephole of the second-finest hotel room in Winnipeg, Manitoba. Squinting, he refocused his right eye and saw a man wearing a crisp, white, collarless shirt standing in the hallway. A black comb and a pair of scissors with long, slim blades protruded from his breast pocket. Lewis continued watching. He did not open the door.

"Are you the barber?" Lewis asked.

"I am," the man said. His accent was Eastern European, although Lewis could not place it more precisely.

"How can I be sure?"

"Listen, I can come back later. Maybe even send someone else? Makes no difference to me."

"No, no. You're right. I'm sorry," Lewis said. He slid off the chain and unlocked the door.

The barber stepped inside. Both men stood in the small foyer. Behind them was a living room of considerable size

45

and a hallway leading to the bedroom and bathroom. Some moments passed.

"Where should I cut?"

"Where's best?"

"Is the bathroom okay for you?"

"Sure. That's fine," Lewis said.

Lewis watched the barber's dress shoes leave prints in the carpet as he walked towards the bathroom. Lewis had never seen a carpet vacuumed so perfectly. He imagined a fleet of miniature snow-grooming machines hiding in the closet, coming out at night to work the carpet as if it were a ski hill. When he opened his eyes, the barber was carrying a chair into the bathroom, and Lewis followed him inside.

Setting the chair on the tiled floor in front of the full-length mirror to the left of the vanity, the barber gestured for Lewis to sit. Lewis sat. Closing his eyes, he felt the barber's massive hands on the sides of his head, turning it this way and that. The barber saw that the roots of Lewis's hair were brown and that it had been cut quite recently, no more than two or three days earlier.

"This hair is very well styled. Very modern."

"Thank you."

"You sure you want me to cut?"

"Very much."

"More conservative?"

"Yes. That's right. More conservative."

"Unlike the suit you're wearing?"

Lewis looked into the full-length mirror, although he did not look at his face. The suit was the height of

46

fashion. As were his shoes and tie. As he stared at his reflection from the neck down, he had the disturbing premonition that his clothes would someday be someone's Halloween costume.

"Yes," Lewis said. "That's it. That's it exactly. The opposite of what I'm wearing."

Lewis felt a towel cover his shoulders. He heard the scissors open above his head. As the barber began to cut, Lewis kept perfectly still.

Many things had happened to Lewis since he'd stood in the middle of an intersection in the east end of Toronto, watching a green-skinned woman pilot a white Honda Civic. The first had been backing away from the limousine he'd been travelling in. The second was climbing inside the nearest taxi.

"Hello," the driver said.

"Yes?"

"Where to?"

"I don't know."

The taxi did not move. Lewis took two twenty-dollar bills from his wallet and, leaning forward, placed them on the passenger seat.

"Straight," he said. "Just go."

The cabbie drove west on Queen Street, and Lewis slumped in his seat, asking himself if he was doing the right thing. The answer came quickly—he wasn't. The right thing would be to go to his wife's funeral and sob uncontrollably. He knew that he should be immobilized with grief. That he should, very shortly, begin raging against a distant and uncaring god. But Lewis was incapable of doing any of these things. Instead, he turned his body slightly to the right and looked out the window.

The taxi drove past buildings that were familiar to Lewis, but he felt as if he had entered an entirely different city. Rolling down the window, Lewis stuck out his head, dog-like. He looked down at the asphalt blurring below him. He turned and looked up at the sky, where an airplane was leaving a long white trail like a line of cocaine prepared and waiting for the crisp, rolled-up twenty-dollar bill.

"Wait," he said. He pulled his head back inside the cab. "The airport. Take me to Pearson."

Already heading west, the cabbie continued on his present course. Two hours later, Lewis was waiting in the designated waiting area at Gate 23, Terminal One, having purchased a one-way ticket to Halifax, Nova Scotia. The rectangular digital clock suspended from the ceiling told him it was 5:43 p.m. Lewis realized his wife's funeral was over by now. He set his watch so it would beep forty-three minutes into each and every hour. Then he presented his ticket to the overly polite airline representative and boarded Flight AC719.

Three hours and forty-six minutes later, Lewis deplaned on the east coast of Canada. Outside the terminal, he took a deep breath. The air that filled his lungs was fresh. He liked this very much, but he knew he couldn't stay. Back inside the terminal, Lewis stared at the departures board. He wanted to travel but lacked any desire to arrive. He purchased a one-way ticket to Vancouver, British Columbia, because it was the longest domestic flight available.

Once in the air, Lewis rested his head against the window and listened to the hum of the airplane. The sound was consistent and made him feel safe. Nothing strange happened until midway through the flight, when Lewis got up and rushed to the bathroom. He did not need to pee. He needed to be alone. In the tiny room, Lewis locked the door and filled the stainless steel sink with water. After several minutes of staring into the top right corner of the mirror, deliberately avoiding eye contact with himself, a slight movement drew his attention.

Looking down, Lewis saw a tiny version of his wife swimming through the water. She wore a green one-piece bathing suit and was 1/98th her usual size. She was perfect in every detail—the black hair, the smile in her eyes, the way she swam the breaststroke, which had always been her favourite.

Lewis pushed his palms against his eyes until he felt like he was falling. "Listen," he said, consciously deciding not to figure out who he was addressing. "I know I'm an asshole. I know I've always been an asshole. But I want to change. I'm willing to change." He lowered his palms and opened his eyes, and when he looked down at the sink, she was gone.

Lewis returned to his seat. At 12:55 a.m., now technically Friday, August 20th, Lewis arrived in Vancouver. He did not leave the airport. He stared at the departures board. The next domestic flight scheduled to leave Vancouver International Airport was flying to Winnipeg, Manitoba. Lewis bought a one-way ticket.

Lewis arrived in Winnipeg at 6:37 a.m., although his watch told him it was 8:37 a.m. He walked past reunions, didn't stop at the luggage carousel, and went directly outside. Standing on the sidewalk, he closed his eyes and listened. Winnipeg felt still, as if it had been unplugged, and this made him feel safe. He had no relatives or friends in Winnipeg. He had never been here before. He had no reason to be in this city. Lewis decided to stay, and he got inside the first taxi in line.

"Take me to the best hotel in town," Lewis said, then he leaned forward between the seats until he could see the driver's face. "No. I want the old hotel. The hotel that used to be the best in town but isn't anymore. I want elegance in decline." The driver nodded and drove him directly to the Fort Garry.

The roof of the Fort Garry Hotel had steep lines in the château style. There were turrets and ornately decorated windows. There was a doorman in a long red coat. There were well-dressed couples entering and exiting. Lewis was surprised to find such a vision of old-world elegance in the middle of the Canadian Prairies. When the doorman opened his door, Lewis decided he would stay forever.

He played with the idea of registering under a pseudonym—perhaps S. Isyphus, or Dr. F. Austus. But in the end he rented the Vice-Regal Suite under his own name. The woman who had shown him to his suite had stood in the middle of the living room, hesitating. She studied Lewis. She nodded her head once she was sure that she recognized him.

"Are you?" she asked, her eyes sparkling.

Lewis did not immediately answer. Raising his eyebrows in an unintentionally comic manner, he reached into the inside pocket of his suit. The hotel employee could not help but notice the thickness of the envelope. Lewis held up a hundred-dollar bill. Pausing, he pulled out a second.

"Not anymore," Lewis said. He held up both bills. The employee nodded. When she'd taken the money, Lewis read the name tag pinned above her heart. "Beth, I'll need a haircut, too."

"I'll make you an appointment."

"Can you send him up?"

"Now?"

"Yes."

"Like, right now?"

"Well, as soon as possible."

"It'll still be a couple of hours."

"Okay, then."

"Is there anything else?"

"I'll let you know if there is," Lewis said, and he closed the door of the Vice-Regal Suite. He went into the bathroom. He filled the bathtub but didn't get in. He pushed down the plug in the sink and filled it too. He sat on the edge of the bathtub, looking from the sink to the tub, then the tub to the sink. But ninety minutes later, when he heard a knock on the suite's door, the miniature version of his wife had still not appeared. Pulling the

drain in both the sink and the tub, Lewis went to answer
the door.

Lewis did not open his eyes until the barber took the
towel from his shoulders. Tiny pieces of hair floated
through the air. Lewis focused on these, consciously
avoiding his reflection in the mirror directly in front of
him. When the barber had finished sweeping up, Lewis
removed the envelope from his inside pocket and took
out two bills. He held these out to the barber.

"This is too much."

"It isn't. You've really helped me here," Lewis said.
He made eye contact with the barber. This was the first
time Lewis had done this. It was the first time he'd made
eye contact with anyone since leaving the limousine.
The barber nodded and took the bills. Lewis walked
the barber to the door of the Vice-Regal Suite and held
it open for him. When he was gone, Lewis locked the
door and slid the chain across. Then he returned to the
bathroom. He stood in front of the full-length mirror.
He took a very deep breath. He looked up, and looking
back at him was someone trustworthy. Someone who was
well adjusted. Someone who hadn't just failed to attend
his wife's funeral.

6

Lewis finds God

Lewis used his teeth to sever the thin plastic string. He put the tags in the garbage can beside the full-length mirror and pulled on the freshly purchased jeans, which were stiff and difficult to button. Pushing with the end of his thumb, he took the toothbrush from its packaging. Remaining shirtless, Lewis began brushing his teeth and was suddenly filled with a sense of comfort, familiarity and home—all three of these sensations caused by a toothbrush.

An hour after his haircut, Lewis had left his hotel room and gone to the Bay, where he'd purchased a complete new wardrobe of clothes in a conservative style, all vastly different from what he typically wore. He'd also bought a razor, deodorant, toothpaste and a toothbrush. It had been quite some time since he'd purchased his own toothbrush, as Lisa had always bought his for him, and unknowingly he had selected one with soft bristles. Lisa had always bought the kind with firm bristles, which was why the toothbrush in his mouth felt broken in and familiar even though it had never been used it before.

Lewis carefully set the brush on the side of the sink. He spat. He walked out of the bathroom and stood over the phone on the bedside table. Picking up the receiver, he pressed a single button and was immediately connected to the concierge.

"I need a garbage bag," he said. "The thickest one you have."

"Certainly."

"And directions to the closest laundromat."

"Would you like to use our laundry services?"

"No, thank you."

"We'll send the directions up with the bag, then."

"Thank you," Lewis said.

The garbage bag arrived fifteen minutes later, and came with a map on which the path from the Fort Garry Hotel to the Happy Cat Laundromat had been traced with a pink highlighter. In the bathroom, Lewis removed the clear plastic from his dress shirts. He pulled out the silver pins, making a small pile on the granite to the right of the sink. He let the cardboard fall to the floor. He removed the tags from the remaining six pairs of pants with his fingers. He pulled the socks apart and plucked off the labels. When he'd finished with the underwear too, Lewis stuffed all the clothing into the black plastic garbage bag and swung it over his shoulder.

In the lobby, Lewis pretended not to notice the desk clerk watching him. He walked through the revolving door, his garbage bag just fitting inside it. Having never been in Winnipeg before, Lewis closely followed the directions on his map. He had just turned left onto Corydon Street when the plastic bag started to tear. The split got longer and longer with each step he took. By the time he arrived at the Happy Cat Laundromat, Lewis was cradling the bag in both arms as he would an injured dog.

Once inside, Lewis fit his newly purchased wardrobe into two washing machines. It took twenty-seven minutes for the clothes to be washed, then he transferred them to two dryers. When the clothes were dry, he put them back in the washing machines. He had just begun his third rotation from dryer to washer when a woman walked into the laundromat. She was fascinatingly unattractive. Her brown hair was dirty and hung just past her shoulders, slightly too long for her face. Her posture was stooped. She did not take steps but shuffled along as if her feet were skis. She was not curvaceous and yet carried too much weight to be thin. Her mouth hung open. There was a mustard stain so perfectly located over her left nipple that it was hard to believe it wasn't intentional. Lewis could not take his eyes off her.

Pretending to stare at the television mounted in a corner of the room, Lewis watched her. She loaded a single washer and then began reading a celebrity gossip magazine. She had removed her clothes from the dryer and was folding an excessive number of pairs of once white, now grey cotton underwear when she looked up, directly at Lewis, then walked towards him.

"Do you know who I am?" she asked, a pair of panties in her left hand.

"Um. No."

"I'm God."

The woman continued to look directly at him. There was no hint of irony or sarcasm in her words. Instinct told Lewis to stop making eye contact immediately and leave the laundromat, but he did neither of these things.

"Really?" he asked instead.

"In the flesh appearing."

"Then I have a question for you."

"Ask me whatever you like, but you have to tell me something first. Why are you doing your laundry over and over again?"

Lewis didn't immediately answer, although he was fully aware that his wife had inspired the repeated washings. Three, maybe four years ago, she'd painted a series of landscapes. They were some of the best work she'd ever done, and certainly the most marketable. Each canvas looked out onto the ocean, a thin line of sandy brown at the bottom leading to a painstakingly rendered sequence of slightly darkening shades of blue.

But then she'd covered them with a sticky lacquer and set them beside an open window. Three days later, she'd returned and the paintings were covered with dust and grime, much of which obscured the subtlety of the many shades of blue.

"Why did you do that?" Lewis asked. Having never succeeded in making anything so beautiful, the thought of her so carelessly destroying it angered him.

"Because I'm so sick of everything being new," she answered. "Of everything looking new. Aren't you?"

Inside the laundromat, Lewis looked up from the floor and into the woman's eyes, surprised by how easy this was to do. "Because I'm sick of everything being new. I want everything to look and feel old."

"Why would you want that?"

"No. Now it's my turn."

The woman bit her bottom lip and nodded almost imperceptibly.

"It's a big one," Lewis said.

"I'm ready."

"Why do bad things happen to good people?"

"Because it makes a good story."

Lewis did not know how to respond. Both her response and how quickly she gave it were unexpected. "That's ... cruel," he said finally.

"You gotta think about it as if you were dead. Because at the end of your life, all you've got is the story of it. If you were guaranteed a happy ending, how satisfied would you be? You'd want some drama! Some intrigue! You'd want to feel that you'd struggled and overcome, even if you'd lost."

"So death just makes a good ending?"

"Works every time," she said. She turned and walked back to her pile of laundry. She carefully folded the last pair of panties. Tucking her basket under her arm, she turned to go. Looking over her shoulder, she caught Lewis's eye. "Take care," she said.

"Oh. Okay."

A dryer buzzed. Lewis removed his dress shirts and then loaded them back into the washing machine.

Just after nine that evening, Lewis wore a very clean dress shirt and a very clean pair of pants as he sat alone in the Palm Room. Although this was his first visit to the hotel bar, Lewis had already fallen in love with it. He loved that the waiters were all middle-aged men wearing white collared shirts and black vests. He loved that their pants were crisply pressed with a crease down the front. He loved that his drinks arrived on napkins stencilled with the hotel's logo and were garnished with cubed fruit on a red plastic sword.

But his deepest affection was reserved for the piano player. The black baby grand sat in the exact centre of the room. Behind it was a grey-haired man with extremely long fingers. His entire body would lean to the right when he played the higher notes, and he would straighten himself out as the melody took him back to the centre. Lewis found himself involuntarily leaning with him.

At the conclusion of a rather trill-filled rendition of "The Girl from Ipanema," the woman from the laundromat sat down at his table.

Lewis nodded.

"You'd never know that shirt was brand new," she said. "Its colour is so dull, and the collar is no longer crisp. It looks like you've had it forever."

"Shh," Lewis said, putting his finger to his lips and pointing at the piano player.

She took the seat beside him instead of the one across from him, and together they watched the pianist work. They did not talk to each other. They ordered drinks between songs but otherwise watched in silence. Lewis found this silence extremely comfortable. The piano player concluded his last set thirty minutes after midnight. At 12:31 a.m. Lewis felt her hand cover his. He did not remove it, and at 12:45 a.m., still without speaking, they left the bar together.

Once inside the Vice-Regal Suite, Lewis went directly to the mini-bar. He looked down at his feet, which left prints in the freshly vacuumed carpet. Removing a tiny bottle of gin from the fridge, he shook it as he crossed the living room. Uncapping the bottle, Lewis set it on the coffee table in front of her.

"One dry martini," he announced and sat down beside her.

"Are you married?"

Lewis had just begun to run his hand through her hair, but he stopped. He looked at his left hand, the ring finger of which still carried his wedding band. "Oh, don't worry," he said. "She's dead."

"Did I just break the mood?"

"A little."

"Recently?"

"Shouldn't you know?"

"It doesn't work like that."

"How does it work?"

"Tell me how she died."

"It was just, you know," he said. He stood up and

walked back across the carpet to the mini-bar. With his head inside it, Lewis continued to speak. "I couldn't find her pulse."

On the morning his wife died, Lewis had decided to let her sleep in. He got the newspaper, made coffee and relished the day's normalcy. Ninety minutes later he went back upstairs to wake her. But she did not wake up. Lewis stood over her, counted to fifteen and then shook her. He checked for a pulse but couldn't find one. Her skin was cold.

He then walked downstairs and began reading the business section of the newspaper. It was the only part of the paper he never read. Tales of mergers, takeovers and investments all felt like secret information, the code of a world he'd never been invited to join. He began reading the stocks alphabetically. He'd reached the Gs when he set down the paper and walked back up the stairs.

In his mind he rehearsed the conversation he would have with her. He pictured her stretching, her arms over her head. *You'll never believe it, he'd say. I thought you were dead*. With a small, embarrassed smile on his lips, Lewis opened the bedroom door, but Lisa was still lying in bed. He checked for a pulse. He still couldn't find one. Sitting on the edge of the bed, he watched daylight brighten the room. He checked once more and then dialled 911. The receiver was still in his hand as he sat down beside her.

"I'm so sorry," he whispered, having already begun to believe that his failure to find a pulse had been what killed her.

Lewis looked up from the carpet and tried to smile. She walked over to him, put her hand over his and squeezed, but Lewis did not squeeze back.

"Really?" she asked. With her other hand she lightly touched his face. Lewis looked down and pulled his hand away. "Lewis, I can't tell you how unique an opportunity this is for you. Can we at least sleep beside each other? That's always nice."

Lewis was struck by her use of the word "nice," which seemed to be without sarcasm or irony. It had been a long time since he'd heard anyone use it that way.

"Yes," Lewis said. "That would be nice."

Holding hands, they walked across the carpet and into the bedroom. They undressed. They climbed into the bed and pulled up the white cotton sheet. Lewis enjoyed the stillness, but then she began violently kicking. He sat up. She kicked and kicked and kicked. When the sheet was untucked from the foot of the mattress, she stopped.

"Why do they do that? It just makes my skin crawl," she said. She was asleep before Lewis could reply.

The next morning Lewis was woken by the sound of a door opening. Surprising himself with his agility, he leapt from the bed. Pulling off the white cotton sheet, he wrapped it around himself and poked his head out of the bedroom. The woman was dressed and was taking the chain off the door.

"Where are you going?" Lewis asked.

"I gotta get to work."

"You have a day job?"

"You sound surprised."

"Being God isn't a full-time gig?"

"Who would I invoice?"

"What's your name?"

"There are so many."

"Tell me."

"Pick one."

"Satan?"

"Come on. Take this seriously. Not many people get to do this."

"Lisa?"

"Not very grand. But okay," Lisa said. She left.

Lewis closed his eyes and listened to the sound of the door as it shut. He heard the brush as the bottom of the door met the frame. He listened to the ridiculously concise melody of the lock mechanism sliding into place. Then he dropped the sheet. He picked up his pants. He was surprised to find that his wallet was still there, with his money inside it. He checked the inside pocket of his jacket, but the envelope remained, seemingly untouched.

PART THREE

Water + Time

Aby 1

7

The theft of a white Honda Civic

Aberystwyth remained crouched behind a red pickup truck on the third floor of the Ultramart Parking Garage, breathing quietly through her gills, as the white Honda Civic pulled into the parking spot three cars away. She waited until the driver was in the elevator, then stood and walked to the car. She kept her arms extended, but her steps remained awkward, and she wobbled on her long green legs.

Awkwardly kneeling at the Honda's back right tire, she reached into the wheel well and slid her hand along the smooth curved metal. Aby had already searched the back right wheel well of every other car, truck and van that had parked in this garage during the last seventy-two hours and found nothing, so her expectations were low. She opened her gills and pushed out a sigh, but then her fingers touched something small and rectangular that was magnetized to the steel. Aby pulled out her arm, and in her hand was a small black box. It took some time before she found the tiny button she needed to push to make the lid open, but when she did she found a key inside.

Aby let out a small cry of victory, her voice reverberating off the concrete walls of the parking garage. With the key in her hand, she approached the driver's door. The webbing of her fingers made it difficult to push the key into the lock, but it turned easily once she got it in. Opening the door was simple, but getting behind the wheel proved more difficult.

The distance between the front of the seat and the pedals was considerably shorter than the length of her legs. Holding on to the roof of the car, Aby curled her right leg underneath the steering column. She sat down so that her knees were on either side of the wheel. She looked at the dashboard. She ran her fingers down from the steering column until she found the ignition. She inserted the key. She turned the key towards her, remembered that she was supposed to turn it away from her and tried again. The engine started.

Having memorized the difference between the symbols "D" and "R," Aby successfully put the car into reverse. She reversed two inches and then stopped. Twisting out of the car, she walked to the back to see if everything was fine. It was. She returned to the driver's seat, curled around the steering wheel and backed up two more inches. She got out to make sure she hadn't hit anything. She hadn't. Aby repeated this process until, seventeen minutes later, she had successfully backed out of the parking space.

Pushing the stick from R to D, Aby turned the wheel all the way to the right, moved a few inches forward, then got out and checked the front of the car. She hadn't collided with anything. She repeated this pattern, gaining confidence as she followed the out signs, but her progress was still punctuated by stops to make sure she hadn't hit anything. On the down ramp there were no cars to collide with, so she made no stops. By the time she reached P1, she was able to drive the twenty feet to the ticket window without interruption.

As Aby approached the kiosk, she was so focused on keeping the gas and brake pedals straight that she almost forgot to cover her gills. This was something Pabbi had repeatedly and emphatically stressed. Looking around, she found nothing that would suffice and resorted to pulling her T-shirt up and over her mouth. There was little she could do about her green skin. A rectangle of paper, which Pabbi had told her was called a parking stub, was in the left-hand corner of the dash. Rolling down the window, Aby stopped and held out the stub. She kept her eyes down but needn't have, as the cashier didn't even look up.

Aby handed him one of the bills Pabbi had given her. The cashier gave her other bills and some coins. A long, skinny barrier in front of her lifted up, and Aby, blinking with excitement, drove forward. It had taken her fifty-seven minutes to exit the parking garage.

Everything Aberystwyth knew about being unwatered she had learnt six weeks earlier, from her father, Pabbi, who lived on the fourteenth floor of an apartment building in an area of town Aby rarely frequented. Late one evening, completely unannounced, Aby had swum to his door and knocked. She felt nervous in the hallway. She knocked again. The door was opened, suddenly and with such force that Aby had to hold onto the door jamb to avoid being pulled inside.

Pabbi wasn't well dressed. He'd gained weight since she'd last seen him. Several seconds passed during which neither father nor daughter said a word.

"I need your help," Aby said.

"Okay."

"I'm going to get her."

Pabbi needed no further explanation to understand who "her" was. "Ah, Aby," he said. "That's ... that's big."

"I know."

"Are you still Aquatic?"

"I am."

"Devoutly?"

"Yes."

"So you're planning on Returning her?"

"I am."

"Oh, Aby," he said.

Pabbi did not move from the door jamb. He looked at the line where the red carpet from his apartment met the grey carpet in the hallway. A window was open in his living room, and the current pushed through the doorway, causing their bodies to sway in unison. The gills in his neck flapped open and he pushed a stream of water through them. Letting go of the door jamb, Pabbi backed into his apartment. "You'd better come in," he said.

With a quick pull of her arms, Aby swam inside. Pabbi

began making a pot of *stryim*. Neither spoke until it had finished brewing. The kitchen table was cleared of dishes, and Pabbi and Aby bobbed around it.

"Why don't you come around more?" Pabbi asked.

"I try."

"Not very hard."

"Will you help me?"

"It's best if you just leave her alone."

"I can't."

"Tell me this—are you going because you want to save her? Or to find out why she left us?"

"Can't it be both?"

"For you, maybe."

"So you'll help me?"

"Have you ever breathed air, Aby?"

"No."

"Walked on legs?"

"No."

"Tried to pass?"

"No."

"It's too much for you."

"Not if you help me."

"Even if I help you."

"I'll do it even if you don't help me," Aby said. She looked up.

"That's probably true."

"Then you'll help me?"

Pabbi pushed a long stream of water from his gills. "As much as I can," he said.

Leaving her at the table, Pabbi swam to his bookshelf.

He pulled down a volume unlike any Aby had seen before. He set it on the kitchen table. Waiting until she was looking over his shoulder, he opened it. The book looked like an atlas, but it didn't illustrate the currents of the ocean. Aby realized that it was a map of land. Flipping through the pages, Pabbi came to an illustration of a large country, coloured pink. He put his thumb on Halifax. He dragged it across the shape, stopping at Morris, Manitoba. Even on the page, the distance seemed enormous.

"It will take you days," Pabbi said.

"Okay."

"Maybe a week."

"Okay."

"And that's only if you manage to steal a car."

"What's a car?" Aby asked.

Pabbi flipped open his gills and pushed a stream of water through them.

It is important to understand that, for devout Aquatics, simply being unwatered is a sin. At the core of the religion is a belief in the Finnyfir, or Great Flood. In this way, Aquaticism is not unlike Judaism or Christianity, but with one central difference: where those religions believe God flooded the world in order to start again, Aquatics believe God simply liked water better.

Aquatic scripture teaches that God found the land imperfect. He thought the mountains were messy, the deserts too dry and the fjords a little showy. He didn't like the way the creatures He'd put on land did nothing but fight amongst themselves. The only thing God liked about His creation was the water. He loved the lakes, rivers and oceans. He loved the way water moved. He loved the colours it came in and the sounds it made. God liked the sorts of creatures that lived in it, and was very proud that it could exist as a solid, a liquid or a gas.

So, after a time, God decided to make it rain for forty days and forty nights, until the world was covered with water. Of course, this killed the majority of the things that lived on land. But as the water rose, a small number of those creatures discovered an ability they hadn't known they had. After the water spilled from the banks of rivers and over the shorelines, after it rose above the roofs of houses and above the tallest trees, when the creatures' fingers could no longer hold the flotsam they'd clung to and the jetsam they'd grasped, they fell beneath the surface and their lungs made the decision for them. Pulling in water as an automatic nervous response, some of them discovered they could breathe it. These creatures, Aquatics believe, were God's chosen. He had given them the ability to breathe the water, leaving all the others to perish.

And perish they did. Land creatures died by the billions. But the Hliðafgoð took up residence below the surface of the water and thrived. Then, after thousands of years, God allowed the waters to recede, exposing the land. God did this to test the Hliðafgoð. Since He had never taken away their ability to breathe air, He wanted to see which of His creatures were worthy of His amphibious gift—and which were not.

God had judged the land to be unworthy; those who

were attracted to it, who would return to it, would be revealed as unworthy as well. This is why the Hliðafgoð had decided—or at least most of them had—to suffer as little contact with humans as possible. Humans were called Siðri, which literally translated means "prone to spit in the eye of God."

While Aquatics believe that it's a sin to breathe the air, it is a minor sin. Within Aquaticism, there is only one sin that is considered an act so blasphemous it is beyond forgiveness, and this is to die with air-filled lungs. This, Aquatics believe, curses your soul to wander disembodied and alone, unwatered and unforgiven for eternity.

But even worse, these damned souls retain all of their memories. They remember everyone they've ever loved and continue to love them just as strongly, if not more so, than when they were alive. Their desire to be with them, to touch them or talk to them, remains eternally unsatisfied. In Gofdeill, the unwatered dead are called the sála-glorsol-tinn, which loosely translates to "famished souls." It was from this fate that Aby hoped to save her mother.

What Aby had going for her was language. When she was still in public school, her mother had made her learn English. Looking back, Aby realized that her mother must have always suspected that she'd one day live unwatered, and had planned on taking her daughter with her. Although Aby's accent remained thick, her vowels were pretty clear and the bulk of the language came back to her easily when she studied it.

Much harder for Aby to acquire were the skills needed to drive. It was easy to understand that the right pedal made the car go, the left made it stop, and it would travel in the direction she turned the steering wheel. More difficult to grasp was the idea that all motion would occur on the lateral plane, whether she was driving, walking or running. It was only after Pabbi suggested she imagine that every space she swam through, indoors or out, had a ceiling exactly as tall as she was that Aby began to understand. But it horrified her.

Aby was also skeptical of Pabbi's advice that she would be able to steal a car by looking for its keys in the wheel well. She did not doubt the existence of cars, or of wheel wells, but the idea that anyone would be so cavalier with their keys seemed ludicrous. Devoted Aquatics, which Aby certainly was, believe that losing your keys not only predicts, but elicits mental illness. To lose one's keys is the equivalent of losing one's mind.

≈

Even as she sat behind the wheel of the white Honda Civic, Aby's keys were close to her, hanging from a string around her neck. As the car straddled Barrington Street, Aby touched her chest, feeling the shape of her keys through the fabric of her T-shirt. She felt comforted. Keeping the left pedal firmly depressed, Aby began searching through her only piece of luggage, a large sharkskin bag resting on the passenger seat.

She rummaged until she found her copy of the Aquatic Bible. Aby flipped through the pages until she found the piece of paper she'd carefully placed between the Book of Doubt and the Book of Endings. Unfolding this paper,

Aby scanned it from top to bottom. She turned it over and did the same. Almost every space, front and back, was filled with handwriting. The letters were very small. The words were very close together. These were Aby's directions. Numbering three hundred and thirteen, they charted a course from the Ultramart Parking Garage in Halifax, Nova Scotia, to the Prairie Embassy Hotel in Morris, Manitoba, a distance of 3,487 kilometres.

Aby pushed a large breath through her gills. She took her foot off the brake. She turned right onto Granville Street; three hundred and twelve directions remained.

The controls of the vehicle were simple, but Aby remained nervous about getting the pedals confused. She came to a complete stop at every corner, the cars behind her honking their displeasure. She had much difficulty matching the symbols on the paper to the symbols on the road signs. She found it impossible to judge the speed of oncoming traffic and whether she was getting too close to the car in front of her.

It took her two hours to find Highway 102, although things got easier once she did. Driving on the expressway was just like swimming with a school: Aberystwyth understood the need to maintain a consistent amount of space between her car and the other cars. After two hours of highway driving, her confidence increased. She leaned back in her seat. She drove with one hand. She was practically relaxed. Then the highway turned from four lanes to two, and suddenly a car began driving straight towards her.

The car did not slow down, nor did it veer from its path. Her first instinct was to make her car go up, but this was something it did not do. She did not go left or right since Pabbi had stressed the importance of keeping the car on her part of the pavement. Aby looked over her shoulder and saw that there were no cars behind her. Pausing briefly to make sure her foot was over the left pedal, she pushed it to the floor mat. Her shoulders hunched. Her legs felt weak. Her skin turned a dark forest green, and she gripped the steering wheel tightly with both hands.

Closing her eyes, she waited. Several seconds passed, but no impact occurred. Surprised, she opened her eyes just in time to see the oncoming vehicle miss hers by inches. Aby breathed out. Her fingers loosened. She turned her head to see the other car receding into the distance. She did not want to continue, but she reminded herself of what was at stake, and then pushed down on the right pedal.

Aby drove without incident for nine minutes, until another car began driving straight towards her. Again, Aby applied pressure to the left pedal. Her shoulders hunched. She covered her face with her hands and watched through webbed fingers as this car, too, missed hers by inches.

Once again, Aby was forced to find new courage. She continued driving. She drove all night. Her fear that every car travelling towards her in the oncoming lane was going to kill her diminished each time it happened. Nine hours later, just past Edmudston New Brunswick, she no longer had to brake when headlights approached. By the time she reached Rivière-du-Loup, Aberystwyth no longer had to stop at the top of hills to check that the road continued on the other side.

8

The unintended consequences of the bi-monthly meeting of the Morris Town Council

Room C-27 lacked air conditioning. The men had removed their jackets and the women fanned themselves with the photocopied agenda. The sweat dotting the mayor's brow, however, was not entirely from the heat. With only one item remaining, the mayor began speaking with greater speed. "Okay, this one should be quick," he said. "It concerns the drought."

The majority of the council members had stopped paying attention some time ago. Mentioning the drought, which was now in its fifty-fourth day, did not bring them back. His next suggestion did.

"I've been looking into ... rainmakers," the mayor said.

Those who hadn't already turned to look at the mayor now did so. A dog, barking some distance away, could be heard. The mayor looked around the table, feeling a sharp need to defend himself. He slapped the table with his open palm. "What do we have to lose?" he asked.

"What does it cost?" Margaret asked as she adjusted the scarf around her neck.

"That's the best part! We only have to pay them if it works. No rain? No pay!"

With this, the room's tone changed completely. A vote was taken and the motion was passed.

"There are two rainmakers who've been recommended. I'll contact both of them. They're a father and son, but I guess there's some bad blood. Maybe we'll be able to play them against each other, increase our odds of success," the mayor said. He and seven of the eight members of the Morris Town Council nodded. Only Margaret abstained, as something inside her, tiny and quiet, began telling her to prepare for the worst.

The towel Anderson was wearing slipped off as he raced to answer the telephone. Naked, he stood dripping onto the phone. He waited for the third ring before he picked up the receiver.

"Yeah?" he said. His feet were getting the carpet wet, which annoyed him.

"Mr. Anderson Richardson?"

"Yes?"

"I'm calling as a representative—"

"Listen, I'm sorry to be curt, but I'm in the middle of something. Is this about rainmaking?"

"Yes."

"Where and when?"

"Ah. Yes. Well. Morris, Manitoba. It's urgent."

"It always is."

"Excuse me?"

"I'll be there as soon as I can."

Anderson hung up the phone, eager to return to his bath. It was only after he'd submerged himself entirely beneath the bathwater and released all the air from his lungs with a long string of bubbles that he realized he had no idea where Manitoba was.

≈

Ignoring the secretary's protest, with his rubber boots squeaking and his raincoat dripping on the floor, Kenneth Richardson burst into the office of the mayor of Charlotte, North Carolina. The sound of rain against the room's west-facing window was persistently loud. The mayor remained seated and calm behind her desk; Kenneth had not trusted this one from the get-go.

"It's raining," he said.

He did not point to the window with either his finger or his head. He remained staring, firmly, at the thin, grey-haired woman who'd served as the mayor of Charlotte, North Carolina, for five consecutive terms. She was a wise, politically savvy woman whose emphasis had always been fiscal responsibility.

"Yes," she said, folding her hands on her lap and returning Kenneth's look with equal intensity. "But how do we know your methods had anything to do with it?"

Kenneth's eye contact intensified. Quickly and without warning, he turned. Water sprayed from his raincoat, landing on the front of her desk. He walked three steps to the window. He saw rain pouring out of eaves-troughs, collecting in puddles, splashing from under the tires of cars. He opened the window two inches, which was enough to let the rain in. It quickly collected on the sill and dripped onto the floor.

Kenneth turned and looked at the mayor but stayed near the window. Reaching behind him, he knocked on the glass three times. Instantly, a small black bird with a bluish head landed on the outside sill. It looked up with yellow eyes and then, with small, desperate movements, struggled to push through the two inches of open window. The bird's sharp, tiny beak darted in and out like a sewing machine needle.

"Are you sure about that?" Kenneth asked.

"We are."

"We did agree on a fee."

"But we have no proof."

"The fee was not excessive."

"We need proof. Do you have any?"

"I understand completely," Kenneth said. He rapped three more times on the window.

Four birds, each identical to the first, landed on the sill. All five struggled to push through the two inches of open window. The mayor was not moved. She leaned back in her chair. She crossed her arms over her chest. Kenneth turned towards the window. Making a knuckle with his index finger, he knocked once, very loudly, against the glass and stepped to the side.

Very quickly there were more birds than the windowsill could hold. The birds fought each other for their positions. They thrust their blue heads through the crack, desperate to enter the room. More birds arrived. More yellow eyes stared through the glass. More tiny beaks pushed through the open window. When there was no more room on the sill, the birds began striking the glass. Each impact was loud. After each strike, another bird took its place. More and more birds began hitting the glass. The number of beaks pushing above the sill seemed innumerable. The window became black, as if night had grown wings.

"Alright! Alright! I'll pay you," the mayor said, her eyes wide and staring at the window. "You'll be paid."

Kenneth, looking at the birds, debated. He needed the money, yet the mayor's fear was giving him considerable joy. For sixty seconds he debated, but then he rapped five times on the window. The birds, all at once, flew away. The room became quiet, with only three sounds remaining: the rain striking the window, the mayor's pen as she signed her name to a cheque and Kenneth's ringing cellphone.

9

The Hliðafgoð

Apart from the fact that they are physically as able to live underwater as they are on land, that their skin is green and changes shade depending on their emotional state, that their fingers and toes are webbed and that they breathe through gills on the sides of their necks, the Hliðafgoð are remarkably similar to humans. They tend to marry for life, although divorce is becoming more and more common, and most straight couples have two or three children.

The Hliðafgoð (the "ð" is pronounced quietly, like the "th" in "rather") have lived in the deepest parts of the ocean for thousands of years. Aby lived in Alisvín-bær (the "æ" is pronounced like "eye"), a city of 2.5 million in the eastern foothills of the Mid-Atlantic Range in the Northern Atlantic Ocean. She'd lived there since she was a teenager, and she liked it fine enough. She found the pace of city life a little too hectic, and the Gulf Stream made the downtown too hot in the summer. The real estate market had recently gone through the roof, leaving her a renter even though she had a good job as a claims adjuster for a large insurance company. Her apartment was small, but not cozy, and was too dark in the mornings. Nonetheless, after twenty hours behind the wheel of the white Honda Civic, there was nowhere Aby would rather have been. Even the scene of the most grisly accident her job had exposed her to had not scared her as much as driving on the 401.

Aby didn't know whether she was nearing Toronto or already in it. It seemed to her that she'd been driving through the same city for an hour and a half. The traffic got thicker, the driving more aggressive, and the three lanes of traffic suddenly turned to six. Just as a seventh lane was added, a red BMW appeared behind her and pulled up so close that she could see the driver's face in her rear-view mirror. Aby was too scared to slow down or change lanes. The BMW passed her on the right and was quickly replaced by a blue minivan. The van drove just as fast and came just as close. Aby increased her speed to 100 kilometres per hour, concluding that she would be safer if she matched the speed of the traffic around her. This was the fastest she'd ever driven, a speed she felt was well beyond her abilities, but she still wasn't going as fast as the other cars on the road.

The blue minivan changed lanes, increased speed and began passing her on the left. At the same time, an eighteen-wheeler began passing her on the right. Both vehicles were travelling only slightly faster than she was. They drove very close to the white Honda Civic, leaving no more than ten inches on either side.

Aby counted the wheels of the truck as it passed her. At six, her gills flicked anxiously. At twelve, she stopped looking and concentrated on keeping the car in the middle of her lane. When the eighteenth wheel went by, Aby pushed out a sigh. The transport truck pulled ahead and then changed into her lane. If not relaxed, she became at least calm, so calm that she failed to notice that she'd merged with the collector lane. She saw exits for streets named Lawrence and Eglinton and Don Mills. Then a sign that told her she was travelling south on the Don Valley Parkway, not west on Highway 401, and Aby began to panic.

She crossed two lanes of traffic to take the Bayview Avenue exit, the next one she came to. She had a choice between Bloor Street and Bayview. She took Bloor because the word reminded her of Bwoor, the Aquatic Saint of Hope. Aby turned left on Bloor, hoping to circle around. She drove over a very high bridge, so high she could see the highway below, and turned right onto Broadview, thinking this would take her there. It didn't. As she drove south on Broadview, Aby became more and more convinced that she was lost. Her gills began to twitch. Spreading the directions across the passenger seat, she hoped to see something that would guide her. When she finally took a quick peek through the front windshield, Aby saw a long black car in the middle of the street and immediately tried to make the white Honda Civic go up, something it still wouldn't do.

"*Myndað af I am að fara til högg ðessi bíll,*" Aby said quietly.

She pressed hard on the right pedal, which made the car go faster. Then, using both feet, she stomped on the left pedal. The tires locked and began to squeal, and an ugly smell filled her gills. Her speed diminished, but the long black car kept getting closer. Aby was so convinced that she was going to crash that she kept her eyes open, concluding that very few people had the opportunity to witness their own demise.

No one was more surprised than she was when the white Honda Civic stopped inches from the back passenger door of the limousine. Aby saw two Siðri looking at her from the back seat of the car. Both had very white skin and seemed to be as relieved as she was. Oddly, Aby was able to feel the woman's relief. They continued to stare at her, their relief turning to shock. Then, quite suddenly, the long black car pulled away.

Aby pushed down on the right pedal. When she'd cleared the intersection, Aby looked in the rear-view mirror. She saw the female Siðri get out of the long black car in such haste that her purse opened and several objects tumbled out. One of these things, Aby clearly recognized, was a set of keys. She kept watching, but the woman did not pick them up.

Wanting nothing but to keep driving, Aby's conscience got the best of her. She tried to tell herself it wasn't her fault that the woman exited the black car so quickly. Keeping her keys safe was her own responsibility. Still, Aby felt responsible. She made her first left and attempted to double back, but she drove into a maze of one-way streets. By the time she'd found her way back to Queen and

Broadview, the limousine was gone. The keys, however, were still on the asphalt, right where they'd fallen.

Aby pulled over. Keeping the engine running, she struggled out of the white Honda Civic and stood on the south side of Queen Street. She waited for a break in traffic. She took her first awkward step off the curb just as a cube van rounded Broadview. Forced to stop, the driver honked his horn. Aby jumped. The van remained still, the driver open-mouthed, as Aby teetered to the keys, bent at the waist and picked them up. With her fist tightly closed around them, Aby turned and staggered back to her car.

Before moving the stick from P to D, Aby examined the key chain. On one side were white letters on an orange background, an "E" next to a "Z." On the other side was a photograph of a group of people—probably a family, Aby guessed. Aby was sitting in the car, looking at the picture and thinking about her own family, when she suddenly became incredibly thirsty. Unbelievably thirsty. Thirstier than she had ever been before. So thirsty that she began to drive, desperately looking for water. A pond, a stream, a puddle—anything would do. As Aby's thirst increased, so did her panic.

Aby drove as fast as she could. Her eyes looked everywhere and at everything. She looked for water on the sidewalks, between parked cars and in third-storey windows. Then, from two blocks away, just as she became desperate enough to try anything, she saw a sign she recognized. The letters "E" and "Z" were in white, set against an orange background. It was the logo from the key chain, and knowing that Siðri needed water too, Aberystwyth pulled into the parking lot of E.Z. Self Storage.

Parking her car, Aby went to the back door because it was the first one she saw. She began sliding keys into the lock, and the fourth one she tried unlocked the door. The handle was different than any she'd ever encountered, very awkward in her webbed hand, but she made it work. Going inside, Aby began searching for water. There was none to be found on the first floor. She couldn't find any on the second floor, either. Keeping to the shadows, Aby returned to the staircase, and on the third floor she found a tiny room in which water dribbled from something silver.

The fact that the tap dripped enabled Aby to recognize its function. Through trial and error, Aby made the water come faster. Aby drank. She pushed her face all the way into the sink and let the water flow directly into her mouth. She plugged the drain with paper she found attached to the wall, waited until a puddle had collected in the sink, then stuck her head and neck into it. Her gills flapped open and she pulled water through them. She breathed. She breathed again. Her thirst was satisfied, but the effort filled Aberystwyth with homesickness. Leaving the tap running, she fled.

PART FOUR

Self Storage

Rebecca II

10

Unit #207

The day after her sister's funeral, Rebecca sat behind her desk in the blood testing lab of Mount Sinai Hospital, doing everything she could not to think about her sister, about the foggy emotions that surrounded her memories of Lisa, or about how these emotions continued to feel further and further away. That her work was repetitive and offered little opportunity for independent thought helped her immensely. After a sleepless night as more and more of her memories became affected, she welcomed the simplicity of running routine tests on blood samples.

Just before noon her telephone rang. It was an external number she didn't recognize, so she ignored it. But ten minutes later, when the same number called again, Rebecca picked up the receiver.

"Blood work."

"Rebecca?"

"Yes?"

"This is Edward. Edward Zimmer."

"Hey. How are you?"

"There's been an accident."

"What?"

"Perhaps it's better if we talk in person."

"I'll be right there," Rebecca said. She hung up the phone, sent an email to her boss describing how severely her sister's death was affecting her and left the lab.

Twenty minutes later she stood at the front door of E.Z. Self Storage. She unwrapped a piece of nicotine gum, looked up at the security camera and tried to smile. The door buzzed and unlocked, and Rebecca went inside.

The office was so sunny that Rebecca could see tiny particles of dust floating through the air. A chest-high counter divided the front from the back, and behind this counter stood Edward Zimmer. His suit was crisply pressed. He ignored her and continued making notes on a thin stack of yellow paper. The scratching of his fountain pen was the only sound in the room.

"Hello, Rebecca," he said finally, setting down his pen. He straightened his tie and smiled.

"Hello, Edward."

Zimmer walked around the counter. He approached Rebecca until they stood very close together. They held hands, mutually squeezing only after their grips were strong. Zimmer raised his left hand and clasped it over the handshake. Other than Stewart, he was the only person Rebecca had ever trusted with the secret of her collection. Somehow it had seemed not only permissible, but necessary, to confess to Edward the true nature of the objects she stored in unit #207. It was a confidence he had never betrayed.

"Good to see you," Zimmer said.

"What happened?"

"We're not sure."

"How bad is it?"

"We don't know," Zimmer answered. He strengthened his grip. "Should we go have a look?"

Taking a deep breath, Rebecca nodded. Zimmer nodded as well, then let go of her hand. Behind the chest-high counter was a yellow door. On this door, stencilled in large black letters were the words EMPLOYEES ONLY. Taking a ring of keys from the front pocket of his pants, Zimmer walked behind the counter. He unlocked the yellow door and held it open. He waited.

"It's okay," Zimmer said.

Rebecca took a half-step and stopped.

"I insist." He waved her forward.

Putting her hands in her pockets, Rebecca walked behind the counter. The carpet ended and her high-heeled shoes made a tapping sound on the concrete. Zimmer followed her, closing and locking the yellow door behind them.

Rebecca was not the only person who rented a unit at E.Z. Self Storage for what Zimmer liked to call "metaphorical purposes." In unit #357 David Glass stored all the objects he'd inherited from his grandmother. These included a hand-carved rocking chair that both he and his wife had seen his dead grandmother sitting in. Unit #111 was rented to Nancy Dixon and contained seventeen mirrors, each of which reflected scenes from what her life would have been like had she made different choices. Unit #438 held a radio that broadcast advice to Steven Moore. Whether it was good advice or bad, Steven didn't know, because he'd always been too afraid to take it.

But as far as Edward Zimmer was concerned, these were not his strangest clients. Far more bizarre to him were those who paid $179.37 a month to store old pots and pans, cheaply made furniture and boxes of shoes decades out of fashion. By contrast, Rebecca Reynolds was one of his most favoured clients. Not only were the items inside her storage space priceless, but she had never been late with her rent, not even once.

The hallway had no window. Fluorescent bulbs lined the ceiling, although most bulbs flickered or were burnt out. Before her eyes had adjusted to the darkness, she felt Zimmer brush by. Rebecca followed, passing equally spaced storage units. All the units had an identical door, and all the doors were painted red and had an identical silver padlock hanging on them. Zimmer and Rebecca walked to the stairwell, climbed to the second floor and stopped in front of unit #207.

Flipping through the keys on his ring, Zimmer cleared his throat. "This is what we know," he said. "Yesterday we had an intruder. I apologize for this. You don't know how sorry we are. We don't know how they got in, or why. There were no signs of forced entry. But for some reason, they plugged the sink in the third-floor bathroom and left the tap running. The tap ran all night. The bathroom in question is directly over unit #208, where there was extensive damage. We can only assume there's been at least some harm to the contents of #207 as well."

Zimmer flipped his keys into his palm. He put the ring back in his front pocket.

"Okay," Rebecca said.

Her second set of keys was already in her hand. She unlocked the padlock, the sound echoing through the hallway. She opened the door of unit #207, and the smell of wet cardboard hit her immediately. She turned on the single bank of overhead florescent lights. The stain started in the middle of the ceiling and flowed to the back left corner. A drop of water was forming at the end of the stain. Zimmer stepped inside the storage space and put his hand on Rebecca's shoulder. Together they looked up, watching the drop become larger and larger. They watched it splash on the top box of the tallest stack in the back row.

"I'll give you some time alone," Zimmer said.

"Thank you."

Rebecca listened to Zimmer's footsteps recede down the hallway. When she was no longer able to hear them, Rebecca began to move boxes, although she did not work towards the water-damaged stack.

Of the hundreds of boxes in unit #207, only eight were not labelled with someone's name. These were all in one stack located in the right-hand corner at the front of the room. The box on top was labelled BIRTHDAYS. The one below that was labelled SEX. The next five were marked FEARS, CRUSHES, FUTURE PLANS, BODY and CHILDHOOD, respectively. The box at the bottom, the largest box in unit #207, read FAILURES.

Stretching her arms over her head, Rebecca grabbed the bottom of the top box in the stack and slid it forward until she could lift it off the stack. She set it on the floor, then removed the boxes marked SEX, FEARS, CRUSHES, FUTURE PLANS, BODY AND CHILDHOOD, leaving the box marked FAILURES standing by itself. Picking it up by the edges, Rebecca tipped it sideways, spilling the contents onto the floor. She pushed through the objects with her toe until she uncovered a ring of keys. These keys had belonged to Stewart. She carefully picked them up and held them in her hand. She closed her eyes.

≈

She stood by the sink in the kitchen of the house she'd shared with Stewart. In her right hand, she held a kettle, which she was filling with water. She hadn't gotten dressed yet. The phone rang and Rebecca answered it, keeping the kettle in her hand and cradling the telephone with her shoulder.

"Hello?"

"I'm sorry."

"Stewart?"

"Yeah."

"Where are you?"

"It doesn't matter."

"Where are you?"

"I'm on my cellphone."

"Where?"

"The bathroom," Stewart replied. "Upstairs."

Rebecca turned back to the sink and shut off the faucet. She walked through the living room and looked up the staircase. She did not attempt to go up, but continued to hold the kettle in her hand.

"I have to leave," Stewart said.

"You've said that."

"I do."

"I know."

"You work so hard to keep your true feelings from me. Do you know how that feels?"

Rebecca walked back into the kitchen and set the kettle on the stove but didn't turn on the element. She pushed the phone closer to her ear.

"Every single failure you've ever had is still with you," Stewart said.

"Aren't yours?"

"No. I have to leave."

"Now?"

"Can you go out for a bit?" Stewart asked.

"How long do you need?"

"An hour," he said.

Rebecca went out for forty-five minutes. When she came back, Stewart's clothes were gone. So were his toothbrush and deodorant and razor. There was no note, although his keys were set precisely in the middle of the kitchen table.

Sitting in the armchair in the living room, her coat still on, Rebecca twirled Stewart's keys in a circle around her index finger. She watched the room get darker and darker. When she finally reached out to turn on a lamp, she changed her mind and went to the door instead. Keeping his keys in her hand, Rebecca drove to E.Z. Self

Storage, walked directly to unit #207 and put the keys in the large box marked failures. It was because of this act, and how quickly she performed it, that no one, not even Stewart, ever knew how much pain, grief and sorrow his leaving caused her.

Rebecca set the keys back inside the box marked failures, then began putting all the other objects back. When everything was assembled, she pulled a white piece of paper from the pocket of her jeans. It was on this paper that Rebecca had written her sister's eulogy, the one focused on the Moving Out memory, which she'd judged useless when those emotions had evaporated. She put it in the box, closed the lid and then restacked the boxes on top in the same order.

Turning, Rebecca looked at the tallest stack in the back row, where the drip continued to land. The stack was almost exactly as tall as she was. Standing on her tiptoes, Rebecca could see the lid sagging on the top box. She tried to open it, but a piece of cardboard came off in her hand. As Rebecca lifted the box off the stack, the bottom sagged. She supported the bottom with her left arm and set the box on the cement floor. It was only then that she noticed the label: LISA REYNOLDS TAYLOR.

Rebecca crouched down and opened the box. Inside were photographs, letters and journals. Everything was from her sister. All of it was paper. The notes in Lisa's handwriting were smeared. The photographs had separated from the paper they were printed on. Ticket stubs were unreadable, and pages of books were bloated.

Every box in the stack was marked LISA ~~REYNOLDS~~ TAYLOR, and all of them were waterlogged.

Rebecca looked back at the open box on the floor, continuing to study the ruined objects until she heard Zimmer's footsteps coming down the hall. Looking over her shoulder, she saw him in the doorway. He carried a red plastic bucket and pulled a large, industrial garbage can on wheels. Stepping into the storage space, Zimmer walked past Rebecca and placed the bucket on top of the Lisa stack. A drop splashed into the empty pail, making a hollow plastic sound. Rebecca pushed her hands under the waterlogged box marked STEWART. She stood up. She carried it out of the storage space and dropped it into the garbage can. She and Zimmer leaned over the top, looking down at the letters and papers that had spilled out of the box.

Rebecca went back inside unit #207, took the red pail off the stack and carried all the boxes out to the hall, dropping them into the garbage can. When she had finished, Rebecca set the bucket on the floor, where it continued to catch the drip. She turned off the light and stepped into the hall.

"It could have been much worse," Rebecca said.

"But it's still sad," Zimmer said.

"It isn't, Edward," Rebecca said, surprising herself. Grabbing the door of unit #207, Rebecca closed it. She locked the padlock. Zimmer put his hand on Rebecca's shoulder. Together, they walked towards the elevator, the plastic wheels of the garbage can squeaking through the empty hallways of E.Z. Self Storage.

11

The taste of forgiveness

Leaving Edward Zimmer to take the water-damaged boxes to the Dumpster, Rebecca drove home and, three blocks from her front door, she felt a pain in her chest. It was severe, but by the time she'd pulled over it was gone. Her hands remained shaky, and she was suddenly quite tired. She felt confident that she could make it home, but her fatigue worsened as she drove.

Having parked her car on a side street behind her house, Rebecca was so tired that she was barely able to unlock her front door, and she fell asleep the moment she reached the couch.

She saw herself sitting at the kitchen table in the Toronto apartment Lisa had shared with Lewis, but whether she was dreaming or remembering was impossible to tell. She was dressed in flannel pyjamas patterned with tiny ducks. They were children's pyjamas, but they fit Rebecca well. She watched as her sister made breakfast. Lisa put two slices of bread in the toaster. She ground beans and began making coffee. Then Lisa put her hands flat against the counter, keeping her back to Rebecca.

"I've decided to forgive you," Lisa said.

The toast popped. Rebecca watched as Lisa smeared forgiveness onto it. She dumped two heaping spoonfuls of forgiveness into a mug and filled it with coffee. Lisa carried the toast and the coffee from the counter to the table, setting both in front of Rebecca. She sat across the table and looked at her expectantly.

Rebecca took a tiny bite of the toast. The forgiveness was very bitter and she could hardly swallow. She took a sip of the coffee, which tasted no better.

"All of it?" Rebecca asked.

Lisa nodded.

Rebecca ate more of the toast and drank more of the coffee. The taste of forgiveness filled her mouth and lined the inside of her throat with something sticky and black. It sat heavily in her stomach. When there was nothing but crumbs on her plate and grounds at the bottom of the mug, Rebecca looked up. Lisa stood and stretched out her arms. They embraced. The hug continued, but Lisa began getting thinner and thinner. Before Rebecca understood what was happening, her sister disappeared.

Rebecca woke up. She could still taste the forgiveness in her mouth. She took off her shoes and socks and put her bare feet against the floor. She sat on the edge of the couch for several minutes, staring at the carpet. She was able to recall her sister's death in two vastly different ways: in one, she thinned until she disappeared; in the other, she died because of a tiny hole in her aorta. Each way seemed equally authentic, but neither made Rebecca sad.

12

The T-Bone experiment

The next morning, Rebecca woke up on the couch with a stiff neck and diagonal lines on her face from the throw pillow she'd slept on. She was already late for work. She showered and dressed quickly. As she stepped into the alley behind her house, en route to her car, Rebecca was surprised to hear a dog barking in her neighbours' yard. The dog was new, but as if prompted by its bark, she remembered the dream in which Lisa forgave her.

With her keys in her hand, Rebecca wondered how she could have believed, even momentarily, that it had been a memory and not a dream. Still, every detail remained as vivid as if it had actually happened: the feel of the flannel pyjamas, the bitter taste of the coffee and the toast, her sister becoming thinner and thinner until she faded away. Rebecca became very sad, and was then overwhelmed by the feeling that something was missing.

The feeling was so strong, and hit her so suddenly, that she began searching her purse for her keys before realizing they were in her hand. She continued looking, easily finding her wallet and her reading glasses. Still the feeling remained. Then the dog barked again, and Rebecca's attention turned to how she was going to get to her car.

Her neighbours were the only house on the block that didn't have a fence between the alley and their yard. This posed a problem, since Rebecca's fear of dogs was profound and she had to pass their yard to get to her car. Taking slow steps, she walked down the alley, past her neighbours' yard. Looking to her right, she saw the dog before the dog saw her. It faced the house and was tied to a tree in the middle of the yard. It had thick muscles where its legs attached to its body, and ripples of skin at the back of its neck.

Sniffing the air, the dog turned and growled. Rebecca's fear grew. The dog's natural ability to sense fear was intensified by Rebecca's natural ability to project her emotions. The dog curled its upper lip and growled again. Rebecca remained still. This had happened before. It happened each and every time she encountered a dog. She knew that her best move was to remain still and assess. Just below the tree the dog was tied to, Rebecca could see several coils of the chain—but the length of the leash was impossible to determine.

Since she did not know whether the dog could reach the alley, Rebecca closed her eyes and pretended she was wearing workboots. The workboots she imagined were tan. They were well worn and steel-toed. Silver lines showed through scuffs at the toe. The lines glinted in the sun as Rebecca lifted her right boot, pulled it back and swung it forward. Boot met dog. The dog's head snapped back. Its lower jaw went left and its upper jaw went right. It yelped.

Opening her eyes, Rebecca looked down. The dog took a half-step backwards and lowered its head. She walked directly in front of it. She reminded herself that in four steps she would be past it. Her feet felt heavy. She took three confident strides, but on the fourth she looked down and saw black Italian leather instead of scuffed tan workboots. Her body tensed. The dog's growl became a loud, angry bark. She heard the chain as the dog begin running towards her. Rebecca looked up. A string of drool hung out of its mouth. Its ears bent back. As its front legs left the ground, it opened its jaws. Squeezing her eyes closed, Rebecca crossed her arms in front of her face.

Rebecca's fear of dogs stemmed from a very specific moment, when she was eight years old and something had barked in her neighbour's backyard. It sounded like a dog, but Rebecca couldn't be sure. She stopped brushing her doll's hair, sat still and listened. The fence separating her backyard from theirs was six feet tall, much too tall for her to climb. However, her house was in the process of being painted, and the painters had left a ladder leaning against the west side of the house. It was long enough that tipping it backwards would put the end of the ladder against the top of the fence.

Rebecca's father had warned her and Lisa not to touch any of the painters' equipment, but when the bark came again, Rebecca became certain it was not the bark of a dog—maybe a tiger, perhaps a wild boar, but definitely something much more extraordinary than an everyday dog. It was something Rebecca had to see. Setting down her doll, she walked up to the ladder. She crawled underneath the bottom step. With her back against the wall of her house, she began to push. It was easier to make the ladder move than she'd expected, although it was also much louder when it fell on the fence.

Rebecca looked up and waited, and when her mother did not appear, she began to climb. Because the base of the ladder had remained relatively close to the house, the arc wasn't steep. It was, however, very wobbly. Twice she almost fell. When she reached the top, she looked over the fence.

The dog saw Rebecca before Rebecca saw the dog. She tried to pull away, but the dog had already jumped. Though she jerked her head back, it was too late; the dog bit into her throat. Or so she thought as her momentum carried her backwards. In truth, the dog had only managed to get hold of her T-shirt, ripping the collar. But Rebecca thought she was mortally wounded as she fell off the ladder, which jiggled, turned and then fell on top of her. She woke up in the hospital with her arm in a cast and a profound fear of dogs.

Although Rebecca put the ripped T-shirt inside one of the growing number of shoeboxes under her bed, it did not trap her new fear of dogs, only her fear of this one specific dog: T-Bone. While it was true that no other dogs or people could feel her fear of T-Bone, this helped little with her fear of dogs in general. It was an important lesson for Rebecca: objects stored only kept the emotions specific to the moment.

Keeping her arms crossed in front of her face, Rebecca heard the dog's jaws snapping shut. But then, nothing happened. When nothing continued to happen, she opened her eyes. The dog's leash was taut. It stood on its hind legs, with its face less than an inch from hers. Its breath was sour. It barked. Flinching, Rebecca took a step backwards. The dog fell to all fours, then jumped back up. It strained against its leash and continued to snarl.

"Fuck you, dog," Rebecca whispered. She turned and walked away. Four steps later, as the dog continued to bark, Rebecca turned around and yelled "Fuck you, dog!" At the end of the alley, she yelled again. "Fuck! You! Dog!" Standing in front of her car, having already unlocked the door, Rebecca stopped and turned around again. "Fuck you!" she yelled. "Fuck you, dog!"

She was in her car, still muttering "Fuck you, dog, fuck you," when she realized that her feelings about Lisa were no longer just foggy; they were absent. Rebecca began sobbing, not for the loss of her sister, but for the loss of every emotion she had for her. Rebecca shut off the engine and pulled the keys from the ignition. She cried for some time.

She continued to sniffle as she drove towards the hospital. As she signalled her entry into the parking lot, she had a thought. Was it possible that her feelings about Lisa had been eliminated when she threw away her keepsakes? And if so, would throwing away any keepsake eradicate whatever emotional history was attached to it? It seemed ridiculous. It was the least likely explanation for the sudden absence of her feelings for Lisa. But realizing that the presence of the dog in her neighbours' yard was the perfect opportunity to test this theory, she turned off her signal and drove directly to E.Z. Self Storage, where she parked and went immediately to the second floor.

Hanging the open padlock on the door of unit #207, she returned to the stack of boxes in the front right corner. She removed the top two boxes and then opened the one marked FEARS. She tipped it over, spilling its contents across the concrete floor. With the toe of her right shoe, she pushed objects out of the way until she found a child's T-shirt with a ripped collar.

Rebecca left unit #207 with the ripped T-shirt in her hand. Opening the back door of E.Z. Self Storage, she went straight to the Dumpster. A plywood bookshelf leaned out of the left corner, and two torn La-Z-Boy chairs were piled on the right. She scrunched up the T-shirt, making a tiny ball of cloth, which she threw into the air. It opened while still going up and then drifted lazily back down towards the middle of the Dumpster.

"Fuck you, T-Bone," she said. "Fuck you."

As the T-shirt landed amidst the trash, Rebecca felt the pain in her heart again, only this time it was much less intense. It was gone before she reached her car. Checking her watch, she saw that less than an hour had passed since she'd left her house. Just after she started the engine, she had a daydream in which she was a child playing in her parents' backyard. Digging in her sandbox, she uncovered a set of miniature dogs. She lined them up in the grass and taught them to bark the national anthem. Again, this felt like a memory, though she knew it wasn't. She'd practically forgotten about it by the time she parked on the side street behind her house and walked back to the alley.

When she reached her neighbours' backyard, the dog was still there, still tied to the tree. Its muscles were just as thick, its teeth just as sharp. Rebecca walked towards it. The dog did not growl or bark. As Rebecca continued to approach, she thought about the moment with T-Bone when her T-shirt had ripped and her fear of dogs had started. Although the facts remained vivid, emotionally it was if the event had never happened. Her fear of dogs had been completely wiped out. This reality was made impossible to deny by the fact that, as Rebecca stood next to the dog, it still didn't bark, growl or snarl. It lifted up its head and, when Rebecca reached out her hand, the dog licked it, its tail wagging.

13

The Prairie Embassy Hotel

There were few, if any, reasons for the Prairie Embassy Hotel to exist. Located three kilometres outside the town limits of Morris, Manitoba, it was not near a major tourist attraction, a natural wonder or even a major highway. The rooms did not have cable; they did not even have televisions. The phones were rotary. There wasn't a computer in the building.

Perhaps Margaret's most antiquated notion as a hotelier was her insistence that the front desk be manned until 2:00 a.m. regardless of how many guests were booked or anticipated. As the hotel's only employee, this task fell to Stewart. So at 12:45 a.m. on Thursday, August 25, when Margaret came downstairs to find out why the phone kept ringing, she should have found Stewart behind the front desk. All she found was his cellphone, which, as she stood there, rang again. Margaret knew that a search of the hotel would likely prove fruitless. There was a much better chance that he was five hundred metres from the hotel, hammer in hand, working on his sailboat.

Stewart sat securing the last of the quarter-inch trim around the cabin, so focused on his work that he neither saw nor heard Margaret as she climbed the stepladder, coming aboard.

"Stewart!" she called, but he still didn't look up. Waiting until his hammer was high in the air, Margaret adjusted her scarf and tried again. "Stewart!"

Startled, Stewart turned, saw Margaret and set down his hammer.

"You sure want to finish this thing," she said.

"I'm so close! Four or five days and it'll be done."

"As long as we don't get any guests?"

"Well . . ."

"It's okay. We probably won't." Margaret kneeled on the deck and then lay flat on her back.

"Do you want me to turn out the lights?" Stewart asked.

"Could you?"

"Of course."

Hanging from the mast were four industrial lamps, each of which was plugged into a long orange extension cord that ran out the back of the hotel and up to the boat. The instant Stewart unplugged the lamps, the sky filled with stars. Stepping carefully around tools and scraps of wood, Stewart lay down near Margaret. Their heads only inches apart, their bodies making a forty-five-degree angle, they stared upwards.

Three years and six months earlier, when Stewart left Rebecca, he did not think he was leaving her forever. He had left her before, on three different occasions, and after a little time to himself he'd always returned to her. But this time was different. Something peculiar happened to Stewart. He experienced a moment of divine intervention while barbecuing.

The house he was staying in belonged to a couple whose recent separation was so painful that neither of them could continue living in their home. When Stewart arrived, he'd been startled by the evidence of quick abandonment: the bed was unmade, mildew-covered laundry filled the washer, and on the kitchen table was a half-full mug of coffee with mould growing inside it. For two days, as Stewart moved around the house, he had the odd sensation that he was on board a ship that had suddenly sunk; the kind of wreck where, years later when the scuba divers discover it, the sails are at high mast, the bunks contain skeletons, and the treasure is still safely locked in the hull.

Just after eight in the evening, Stewart checked the freezer, because cooking felt like less effort than talking to a deliveryman. He was more than a little drunk, having discovered the liquor cabinet earlier in the day. Finding a stack of seemingly inseparable patties, he carried them to the backyard. The problems began when he discovered that the barbecue was not gas but was filled with charcoal. Remembering childhood barbecues with his father behind the grill, Stewart searched for a can of lighter fluid. Finding one, he squirted a liberal amount of fuel on the coals.

Stewart went back to the house and returned with a box of wooden matches. He opened the box without realizing it was upside down. The majority of the matches fell through the grill and onto the coals. Lighting one of the few that remained, Stewart dropped the match. The sudden whoosh made him close his eyes. Putting his hands to his eyebrows, he confirmed that they were still there. When he opened his eyes, Stewart saw what seemed to be dangerously tall flames rising from the barbecue. The flames did not get bigger or smaller. They seemed to burn without consuming anything. In the centre was a tiny blue flame that flickered higher and lower as it spoke.

"You know as well as I do that she has to ask you back," the tiny blue flame said. His voice was kindly and familiar. "And she has to voice it. She has to say it out loud. And what she's saying underneath it, what she's saying with her heart, has to be the same."

"That would be nice."

"But has she ever done it before?"

"No."

"Not once?"

"No, not once."

"So it's pretty obvious that you're gonna have to wait for her to say it, no?"

Stewart became suspicious. "What are you getting at?" he asked.

"I mean, you could go back to her, but where's that gonna get ya?"

"Right back here."

"Exactly. That's all I'm saying. You're gonna have to wait."

"I guess so."

"So while you're waiting, here's something you can do. A noble cause. A personal quest."

"Is this a vision?"

"Call it what you want."

"What? What do you want me to do?"

"Go west."

"And?"

"Maybe build a boat?"

"Maybe?"

"The rest is up to you."

"Come on!"

"Sorry, but that's as specific as I can get right now," the tiny blue flame said. It got smaller and disappeared.

Stewart stood there for a second, failing to notice that the flames had suddenly gotten higher and hotter and that the white vinyl siding on the house was turning black. He threw his drink on the fire, which only made the flames spurt higher, then he spotted the garden hose.

The next morning, Stewart drove to Home Depot and purchased seventeen feet of vinyl siding. Still hung-over but having completed the repairs, he called Rebecca to make plans for his return. But when they talked, Stewart could not feel her heart. Or, at least, he felt no sadness, grief or loss coming from her—neither her voice nor her heart asked him back.

Stewart headed west and, through a combination

of chance and cheap bus tickets, arrived in Morris, Manitoba. He'd planned on spending a single night at the Prairie Embassy Hotel, but the next morning, purely on impulse, Margaret offered him a job as night clerk. Stewart accepted, agreeing to a three-month contract.

It was during the first month of his long, lonely nights at the front desk that Stewart began to wonder if the flame of the burning barbecue really did have a divine origin. He began to set small, controlled fires in an effort to seek advice and wisdom—and sometimes simply out of loneliness. It never worked, so Stewart began to suspect that only an accidental fire would make the tiny blue flame speak to him again. But accidentally setting a fire was difficult to do.

However, three weeks after his arrival in Morris, he began building a sailboat. Although he wasn't entirely convinced that the tiny blue flame had been divinely inspired, he figured, why chance it? He had a lot of time on his hands. Things at the Prairie Embassy Hotel were slow, and Stewart was a man who liked to stay busy. Plus, he estimated that he could get the whole thing built in under three months, easy.

Stewart and Margaret continued staring upwards, neither moving nor speaking. Both had been lulled into a contemplative state by the innumerable stars overhead. After more time passed, Margaret spoke. "How metaphorical do you think this boat is?" she asked.

Propping himself up with his left arm, Stewart looked

at Margaret. She continued looking up at the sky. "What are you asking?" he asked.

"Can I be frank?"

"When aren't you?"

"This requires a greater degree of frankness than usual."

"I'll tell you if I think you're going too far."

"That's fair," she said. She spoke directly but continued looking up at the stars. "Do you think this boat, the building of it, is misplaced anxiety about leaving Rebecca? About how badly you want to leave her—emotionally, not just physically—but you can't?"

Stewart did not immediately reply. He tapped the toes of his workboots together. He looked up at the mast, which he saw as a long, thin absence of stars. Making a knuckle with the index finger of his right hand, he tapped the deck three times. "That's a lot of misplaced anxiety," he said.

"The only other explanation I can think of is that you feel fated, or called upon, to build a sailboat in the middle of the Canadian Prairies."

Once again Stewart's reply was not immediate. He patted his pockets and realized that he'd left his phone in the hotel. He sat up halfway, so he could see Margaret's face, and then lay down on the deck again. "I see your point," he said.

"So which is it?"

"Can it be a little Freudian as well?"

"A little *whatian*?"

"Could it be that you're also obsessed with this boat?"

Stewart asked. "So much so that you keep me employed, even though you have no need for me, because you see this boat as a metaphor for yourself? That you are, in fact, a sailboat stranded in the middle of the Prairies?"

"Oh, that's good."

"Thank you."

"But which is it?"

Sitting up, Stewart took off his shoes and socks and then lay back down. "Isn't it kinda the same thing?" Stewart asked. "If I hadn't met Rebecca and fallen in love with her, and then left her, I wouldn't be here, and I wouldn't be making this boat. So the boat wouldn't exist and neither would your question. Was it fate that I fell in love with Rebecca? And then that I left her? Or that I loved her, left her and then found this place and started building this boat? What's fate and what isn't? Where does it stop and where does it start? Is fate part of the story or the whole story?"

"Well, which is it?"

"I don't know. What about with you?"

"We're different because I managed to leave everything. And I think I left even more behind than you did."

"Like what?" Stewart asked. He closed his eyes, knowing that a long pause would follow.

Even though they'd worked side by side for three years, Stewart knew very little about Margaret. What he did know had come slowly, during quiet moments exactly like this one.

When Margaret finally did speak, her voice was uncharacteristically hushed and soft. "I left a husband

and a daughter. The husband I don't think about much; he rarely crosses my mind. But my daughter, I think about her every day. She was so young that I was never able to explain to her why I had to leave. I haven't seen her or talked to her since. It was her birthday on Wednesday."

Stewart did not know what to say, and he cared enough about Margaret to say nothing. Reaching out his hand, he touched her gently on the shoulder. Margaret leaned towards this touch, and for some moments they were quiet, the only sound a transport truck on the highway far away. Then, with a quiet intake of air, Margaret stood up. "Anyway, that's not what I'm here for," she said.

"You want me to stop hammering?"

"Why would I want that?"

"It's after one in the morning?"

Margaret laughed. She stretched out her arms and turned in a circle. "Who would you be keeping up?"

"You?"

"That's not what's keeping me up. No, you left your cellphone at the front desk. It's been ringing all night and driving me crazy. Somebody's really trying to get a hold of you," Margaret said. She pulled out his phone and handed it to him.

"Thank you."

Margaret climbed down the ladder, stopping halfway. "Be nice, but don't be too nice," she said.

Stewart had already begun dialling Rebecca's number.

14

All things Stewart

Rebecca had been sitting in her car for hours, watching bugs circle the streetlight in the parking lot of E.Z. Self Storage. She opened the door just far enough that the overhead light went on and the warning signal pinged. She looked at her cellphone resting on the dashboard and was surprised when it began to ring. Without checking the caller display, she answered it. "Stewart?"

"Hey," Stewart said. "How are you? How'd it go?"

Rebecca closed the car door and was in darkness again. "What would you do if you could walk away from your past?" she asked.

"Wait—what happened with the eulogy?"

"It was very bad. Terrible. But something new has happened. Just listen."

"Okay."

"If you could, would you walk away from your past?"

"Rebecca, I did walk away from my past."

"Then why are you calling me? It must be, like, after one in the morning there."

Stewart had no reply to this. "Why are you asking me this?" he finally said.

"Just play along. Please? Pretend something magical happened and you suddenly had the power to emotionally detach from your past. To make it all evaporate, completely. Would you do it?"

"Is it all or nothing?"

"What do you mean?"

"Do I have to get rid of all of my past? Or can I pick and choose?"

"That's it."

"What is?"

"You're saying I could just pick what I want to get rid of, the stuff that's making me stuck—stuck in the past—and leave the rest."

"Isn't this hypothetical?"

"It's perfect."

"Rebecca?"

"Thank you so much."

Rebecca closed her phone. She got out of the car. Using the key Zimmer had given her, she entered E.Z. Self Storage through the loading bay door. The lights flickered in the sluggish elevator, making her wish she'd taken the stairs. When the doors opened, she ran as fast as she could. She was out of breath when she reached unit #207. She inserted the key into the lock and twisted. She put her forehead on the door and stood perfectly still.

For three years, since Stewart left her, Rebecca had

felt that her life had been ruined by how much she'd loved him. But no matter what she did, she couldn't get rid of that love. She did not know what would kill it. Both neglect and abandonment had failed. Its survival, Rebecca believed, was due to her unchanging life, which trapped her in the same moments again and again, as if time were hiccupping. But now she had a way out. Her toes curled in her shoes. She took three very deep breaths and then pulled the padlock open.

Inside, Rebecca began to search for the boxes marked STEWART. She had divided him into a large number of tiny boxes, the majority of which were on the left, about three rows back. She found a box marked STEWART—SINCE DIVORCE. Beside it was STEWART—HOUSE ON WATER STREET. The three below that were all marked STEWART—WEDDING. She found a box marked STEWART—FIRST APARTMENT and two that were labelled STEWART—DATING. Soon she had located them all.

Rebecca carried all of these boxes out of her storage area and set them on the concrete floor in the hallway. She walked down to the main floor to get the dolly. She took the elevator back to the second floor. She pushed the dolly to unit #207 and began loading the boxes.

Even fully loaded, the dolly was easy to move. It fit easily into the elevator. She rode down to the first floor, where she pushed it out the back door and down the ramp, stopping in front of the Dumpster. Without hesitating, Rebecca opened the Dumpster and began throwing boxes inside. Some of the boxes made a loud crash when they landed. Others made a dull thud. Rebecca found both sounds extremely satisfying. When there was only one box left, she threw it as high as she could, watching it rise up into the air and then crash into the Dumpster. Rebecca closed the lid and stood silently in front of it.

The pain in her chest came quickly. It was severe and sharp. She doubled over and collapsed onto the ground. She brought her knees up to her stomach. She tasted bile in the back of her throat, but she did not throw up. The pain stopped as quickly as it had started.

Standing up, Rebecca brushed the dirt off her pants and, without looking back at the Dumpster, walked to her car. Driving home, she became overwhelmed with fatigue. During the twenty-minute trip, she felt the need to pull over twice. Both times she had to get out of the car and walk around it twice before she felt ready to continue.

Parking in front of a fire hydrant, Rebecca barely made it to her house. She lay down on the couch and began dreaming, or remembering—she couldn't tell which. She saw herself in bed with Stewart. Shortly after waking, they sneezed at exactly the same time. Both sneezes were forceful: so forceful that Rebecca blew her personality into Stewart and Stewart blew his into Rebecca. Neither immediately noticed that anything unusual had happened. Stewart rolled out of bed and went to the bathroom. Rebecca reached for the Kleenex on her bedside table and discovered that she was on the wrong side of the bed. The right side was usually hers, but being on the left side wasn't particularly odd. It had happened before. When she put on her housecoat, she found it tight, but not so tight that she was alarmed. But then, looking at her hands, she saw that they were large and masculine. They didn't look like her hands at all. She was still staring at them when she heard a scream from the bathroom.

The scream was odd because it sounded exactly like her voice. Rebecca went to investigate and saw herself coming out of the bathroom. This made her scream. The scream that came out was not her voice, but her husband's voice.

"Stay away from me," Rebecca said.

Stewart raised his hands, open-palmed, noticing that his nails were long and painted. "Rebecca?" Stewart asked in Rebecca's voice.

"Stewart?" Rebecca asked in Stewart's voice.

They exchanged housecoats and wondered what they should do. Craving normality, they went downstairs and started breakfast. Rebecca made eggs. After they'd eaten and cleared the table, Rebecca suggested that they might as well make the best of it.

"Wouldn't that be ... gay?" Stewart wondered.

"More like self-abuse."

"It is tempting."

They went upstairs to the bedroom. It was over quickly. Afterwards, they stared up at the ceiling. Neither of them had found it that arousing.

"It must have been the sneeze," Rebecca said.

"That's what I'm thinking too."

They headed back to the kitchen, where Rebecca took the pepper shaker from the back of the oven. They both sniffed. The pepper made them sneeze. The sneezes were intense, but it was hard to get the timing right. On the seventh try, they managed to sneeze simultaneously. Stewart blew his personality back into his body and Rebecca blew her personality back into hers.

"Weird," Stewart said, happy to be back in his own body.

"Very," Rebecca agreed.

They hugged, showered, got dressed and went to work. They pretended that nothing had changed. They continued to pretend when they returned that evening. But something had changed. Touch had become something they had to think about, and each time they had to think about it the less inclined they were to do it. In four days it became impossible, and in four weeks they'd drifted so far apart that Rebecca couldn't find Stewart anywhere. She looked in every room, under every bed and inside every closet, but he wasn't in the house.

Rebecca woke up frightened. She was filled with anxiety and a desperate feeling that something very important was missing. She got off the couch and began searching for her keys, which she found on the kitchen table. She searched through her purse and found her wallet near the top. Still, the feeling that something was missing would not go away.

Taking short, shallow breaths, she stood in the middle of the kitchen. Hoping it would relax her, Rebecca decided to shower. She had just covered her hair with shampoo when she realized that she didn't know what time it was. Fearing that she was late for work, she rushed to the kitchen. Dripping on the linoleum floor, she looked at the clock on the microwave, which read 5:47 a.m. The shower continued running. Rebecca sat down, her skin slipping on the vinyl kitchen chair. Twenty minutes later, stuck to the chair, she realized that what she was missing was the missing of Stewart.

PART FIVE

Vatn Auk Tími

Aby II

15

The windshield cracks

Aberystwyth was driving north on Highway 400, two hours outside of Toronto, and had just passed Wood Landing when a stone flew out of the gravel truck in front of her. It cut through the air so sure of itself, as if it already knew where it was going. She had never before seen an object move like this. The stone displayed so much confidence. She stared at it, envious, studying its progress. Then it struck her windshield, creating an elliptical chip and scaring the hell out of her.

Aby clasped the steering wheel until her knuckles were lime green and used both feet to push down on the left pedal. She pulled onto the shoulder while the car still had considerable speed. When the white Honda Civic became motionless, so did Aby. A large transport truck passed, causing the car to shake. Lifting her trembling index finger, Aby touched the chip. Her skin turned dark green. She had not known glass could break, and she suddenly felt extremely vulnerable inside the white Honda Civic.

Aby got out of the car, supporting herself with the open door, and surveyed the horizon. Directly in front of her was a field where cows were chewing grass and ignoring her. Looking past them, Aby focused on a maple tree that stood by itself in the middle of the field. Taking tiny steps, she walked down the small hill between the highway and the field. She noticed a series of short wooden posts standing two or three feet apart. A thin line of string connected them. It looked like the string would cause little resistance, but when she touched it, a sting more painful than that of any jellyfish went through her. Aby let go of the string. She looked at the fence. She touched it again, this time grasping it firmly, which only made the sting more painful.

Aby looked around and noticed the tall wooden poles that lined the highway. Aside from the maple tree, these were the tallest objects in sight. She crawled up the hill and made her way to the nearest pole. The poles were connected by strings far above her head. Tentatively Aby reached out her hand and lightly touched the pole with her index finger. When she felt no sting, she pushed a breath of air through her lungs, lowered herself onto her back and shimmied her body until the top of her head was firmly against the pole.

When Aquatics are overwhelmed, they seek out the tallest object in view, lie on their backs, put their heads against it and look up. The ritual is called *lítill*, and its purpose is to remind believers that they are actually quite small and, therefore, so are their problems.

Craning her neck, Aby looked up to the very top of

the pole. While the height of the pole did make her feel small, she had to stare for some time before she began to believe that her problems were also small. She continued to stare. Then, knowing that if she didn't get back inside the white Honda Civic soon she never would, Aby stood. Her steps were stumbly, but she did not fall on her way back to the car.

Starting the engine, Aby ignored the sick feeling in her stomach, put the car in gear and depressed the accelerator. The white Honda Civic gathered speed on the shoulder. Looking at the side-view mirror, Aby saw a car approaching. She still found it extremely difficult to judge the speed of objects in the distance. The car looked small in the mirror, so she pushed the gas pedal to the floor. The engine made a high whiny noise. The tires spun in the gravel. She found steering difficult. The speedometer told her that she'd reached a speed of 60 kilometres per hour. Aby knew it needed to read 100. In the rear-view mirror, the car behind her continued to approach with great speed. Her speedometer read 80 and she decided this was close enough. She jerked the steering wheel to the left. As the tires grabbed the pavement, the car began to swerve.

The white Honda Civic veered through both lanes, and Aby heard the left wheels go into the gravel. The tires slipped as small rocks hit the inside of the wheel well. Her right wheels remained on the road. A car behind her grew large in her rear-view mirror. She depressed the right pedal, but the white Honda Civic would not go faster.

Hunching her shoulders, Aby closed her eyes and heard a horn honk in one long monotone.

There was no impact. Opening her eyes, Aby watched the car, now in the right lane, speed ahead. In her panic, she hadn't anticipated that the vehicle would simply go around her. Slowing down, Aby steered to the right until all four wheels rolled on the asphalt. Feeling that immediate danger was over, she refocused her eyes on the chip in the windshield. It was at this point that the off-ramp for Exit 168 came up, and Aby, having no idea where it would take her, took it.

This was the first time she had chosen to deviate from Pabbi's directions. Her fingers ached when she relaxed her grip on the steering wheel. Once off the freeway, she continued to drive without a destination, choosing roads that took her away from any buildings, and at 5:57 p.m. Aby passed a river. She decided that this was where she would spend the night. She pulled over.

Opening the door, Aby turned sideways in the seat. Her legs were so stiff that she had to use her hands to move them. She stretched them outside the car. With the rest of her still inside, she pulled off her pants and her underwear and her shirt. Taking tiny steps, Aby walked towards the river. The ground was uneven. She stepped onto the edge of a rock and was knocked off balance, which forced her to take another step, which caused her to take another, which caused her to fall. But she was close enough to the river that she fell forward into it, and the instant she hit the water, her grace returned.

Aby submerged. She performed a series of somersaults.

She swam with the current and built her speed, caressing the rocks as she swam around them. She tacked against the current and then, spinning on her back, hovered just beneath the surface. She opened and closed her gills. She pulled fresh water deep into her lungs for the first time.

Pabbi had said that her biggest challenge wouldn't be breathing air, or the distance she'd have to travel, or the driving or even her colour (the longer she stayed out of salt water, the more her green would fade). It would be her legs. He warned her to stretch them as much as possible, but not to push them and never to trust them. Aberystwyth had not listened.

As she continued to float just below the surface of the river, Aby's greatest fear wasn't for her soul but for her legs. She was overcome with sadness: this was decidedly not how she'd intended to spend her forty-first bithday.

16

Ást

According to the Aquatic Bible, the only holy objects in the unwatered world are clouds. There are three reasons for this: the first is that clouds never touch the ground; the second is that clouds are the source of all water; and the third, and by far the most important, is that when a Hliðafgoð dies, their *upplifa*, or soul, evaporates and travels as vapour into the clouds. Once inside a cloud, an *upplifa* begins absorbing its characteristics. When the soul falls back to earth in the form of rain, the life it enters is greatly influenced by the type of cloud the *upplifa* falls from.

That is why, on the morning of Tuesday, August 23, when Aby woke up in a river she could not name, with fresh water filling her lungs and clouds drifting overhead, she instantly began contemplating her death. Floating just under the surface, she watched the clouds floating slowly above her and thought about what it would be like to be reborn from those clouds. They were small and compact, and Aby thought she'd like that, being a personality drawn to small, compact things. She took a large amount of water into her lungs, then pushed it out through her mouth, breaking the surface and making a fountain of herself.

"*Vatn auk tími*," she said. "*Vatn auk tími*." This phrase, often repeated by Aquatics, is used in a variety of situations to mean a number of different things. Literally translated, it means "water plus time." But there is an implied understanding that the phrase "nothing can resist" precedes the statement. So, during times of stress, it can be said to remind the believer that the difficulties they're having are temporary. It can also be used when beginning a task that appears insurmountable. But by far the most common use of the phrase is to acknowledge that what happens in your life is mainly out of your control, that bigger forces are at work, and resisting their influence is useless.

Aby began climbing out of the river. It was much more difficult than she anticipated. Her legs were too weak to be of much use, and there was little for her hands to grab hold of. Hip-deep in water, Aby waded three hundred metres downstream to a place where the banks were lower. She crawled from the water and sat on the shore, dreading having to take her first breath of air. She held her breath for as long as she could, then her gills opened and contracted, and she felt the dry air inside her.

When she finally got back to the white Honda Civic, she did not feel like she could get inside it. Reaching out, she put her index finger against the chip in the windshield. Its texture remained rough, but from the outside it felt more like coral. This association allowed Aby to persuade herself that the chip couldn't be that bad, that driving the car would be okay and that death, while still likely, wasn't certain.

Aby placed a long leg on each side of the steering column. She turned the key towards her, then remembered to turn the key away from her. She began trying to find the highway. After more than forty minutes of random turns, she found a secondary road that led her to an on-ramp. Although she could not bring herself to reach the posted speed limit, Aby drove without incident for hours. Then, forty-five minutes outside of Thunder Bay, eighteen hours away from Toronto, extreme thirst struck her once again.

Seeing a large collection of tractor trailers parked beside a one-storey building very close to the road, Aby left the highway. She parked the white Honda Civic and staggered towards the building. She walked as if she were drunk, although the opposite was true—it was drinking too little that caused her to sway.

Aby became convinced that she had only moments to find water. Having never witnessed dehydration, Aby could not fathom how it happened. She pictured every cell in her body shrivelling, her skin suddenly becoming many sizes too big, then crumbling and blowing across the parking lot. With these thoughts in mind, Aby was understandably anxious as she threw open the glass doors of the building.

Until this moment, Aby had been careful never to interact with large groups of Síðri. Now she felt she had no other choice. She stepped inside. As her eyes adjusted to the relative darkness, her gills nervously flared open and closed. Her eyes searched for water. She was concentrating so intensely that she was able to ignore how the sound of food cooking was suddenly audible, how all movement within the restaurant had stopped, and how the majority of the patrons, mostly men wearing trucker hats, were staring at her.

She saw bottles of water only three paces to her right, in a box as large as she was. Aby reached her hand through a rectangular hole close to the bottom. She twisted her arm and pushed her hand farther up, but the bottles remained untouchable. Large, square buttons covered the left side of the box. Aby pressed each button, then pushed them in a variety of combinations. This produced no results, which caused her frustration to grow. Ignoring the Síðri, who continued to stare, and curling her hand into a fist, Aby struck the side of the machine. The bottles didn't fall. She hit the machine again, harder, but the bottles remained standing. Then, remembering the small stone flying through the air and the resulting chip in her windshield, Aby pulled her arm back. She aimed. Using all her force, Aby threw her fist at the front of the machine—but it stopped an inch from the glass.

Initially Aby couldn't understand why her arm had ceased its forward motion. Seeing the hand holding her wrist only increased her confusion. That a Síðri had more strength than her was impressive. She followed the hand to an arm and the arm to the face of a man slightly taller than her, and much taller than most of them. His eyes were green and his skin had a greenish hue.

Continuing to hold her arm, he deposited a series of coins through a slot that Aby hadn't noticed. He pressed the upper left square. The machine whirred. A bottle of water fell down into the rectangular hole, and then he let go of her arm.

Aby grabbed the bottle, opened it with her teeth and drank the contents in a single pull. The man put in more coins. He pressed the button again. Another bottle fell. Again she used her teeth to open it, and again she drank it in a single swig. Six bottles later, Aby looked up at him. "I veed mowre," she said.

"*Ég don't hafa allir fleiri breyting.*"

"*Ekki a Hliðafgoð?*"

With this he took off his scarf and flared his gills. "Ást."

"Aberystwyth."

"*Við öxl fá út af hér!*"

The bluntness Ást had used to describe their situation pulled Aberystwyth out of her joy at seeing another of her kind. She took her first good look around the truck stop. The patrons continued to stare. She sensed that their disbelief would soon turn to fear. Although Aby was standing 210 metres above sea level, breathing air, her skin flaking from the dryness, she was, for the first time in her life, in over her head.

Aby scanned Ást from his feet up to his undeniably handsome face and decided that she could trust him, although in truth there was little else she could do. "*Hvaða öxl við gera?*" Aby asked.

"*Keyra!*"

Aby nodded, and they began to run, fleeing the truck stop together.

An Aquatic will never question anything that happens by chance. In fact, the greater the coincidence, the more an Aquatic believes it was meant to be. This concept is called *vilja*, which translates as "God's cheat," the idea being that what appears to be chance is how God influences the plot of your life. If something extremely improbable happens by chance, it wasn't chance at all, but God's hand arranging the events of your life to meet the divine will.

The concept of *vilja* is very closely related to that of *tibrt*. Literally translated, this means "current-move-time." A more poetic translation would be "river season," since at the bottom of the ocean, currents move like rivers.

Aquaticism teaches that there are five seasons. *Fins*, when things grow, is like the Síðri summer. *Gsll*, when things wither, is like fall. *Virth*, when things sleep, is like winter, and *zre*, when things begin again, is like spring. The fifth season, the one the Síðri don't believe in, is *tibrt*, the river season.

The river season is the time when you must enter a current and be taken to some new place, the place you're supposed to be—the place you're fated to be. A river season could happen at any moment. You could experience a river season three times a year or not at all for thirty years. It could happen to you but not to whoever is sitting next to you.

But most importantly, a river season will last as long

as it takes you to reach your new place. If you get into the river and let it take you where you need to be, your river season will last an afternoon. But if you fear change and struggle and hold on to the rocks, the river season will last and last. It will not end until your body becomes exhausted, your grip weakens, your hands slide off the rocks and the current takes you to your new place.

Aby's thoughts were not on river seasons, although maybe they should have been, as she untangled herself from Ást's bedsheets. She was more focused on, and impressed by, her increased ability to walk on land. When they'd fled the truck stop, Aby had run, if not exactly quickly, then without falling and with only small amounts of wobbling. This was a large improvement in just eight days of being unwatered. Aby couldn't help but feel proud of herself.

Remaining in bed, Aby surveyed the room that she believed *vilja* had directed her to wake up in. She saw Ást's wallet on the bedside table and the black shirt he'd been wearing hanging over the back of a wooden chair. There was a small pile of change on his dresser and a half-open drawer that looked to be full of socks. Aby was amazed at how perfectly he was living Síðriin, and how easy it seemed to be. She realized for the first time in her life that it was, at the very least, an option, and this thought made something inside her speak. She had not consciously known she had any desire to live this way. Before this desire could grow, Aby pushed it down and got out of Ást's bed.

Normally not of easy virtue, Aby had been easily

seduced, fuelled by loneliness, propinquity and a fear that the end of her world was near. From the moment Aby had stolen the white Honda Civic, she had been convinced she would die in it. She was so sure a fatal accident lay ahead of her that she thought of each passing kilometre as bringing her not closer to the Prairie Embassy Hotel and her mother, but nearer to the collision that would kill her, a death she believed would transform her soul into a *sála-glorsol-tinn*.

With these thoughts in her head, Aby felt the need to crawl back into Ást's bed. She got under the covers, wrapped as much in the feeling of calm and safety as in the cotton sheets. For twenty minutes she felt at peace and without fear, but then at minute twenty-one the guilt set in. Aby did not try to fight it. With a shake of her head, she pushed a small sigh from her gills and began to hunt for her clothes. She had dressed and was opening the front door when Ást, wrapped in the bedsheet, caught her.

"You already want to leave?" Ást said. He spoke in Hliðafgoðian, and for the first time Aby noticed that his pronunciation was perfect, his accent distinctly upper-class.

"I need to keep moving," Aby responded, suddenly feeling slightly ashamed of her accent.

"Please stay."

"I can't."

"Just for breakfast?"

Aby shook her head.

"Then I'll take a look at your car, the engine, the brakes, everything. I'll make sure it's safe."

Aby decided she couldn't leave yet. She closed the door. She promised herself she would only stay three more hours, then get back on the road. She followed Ást, although his path was not towards the kitchen.

Six hours later, Aby could only see Ást's feet. The rest of him was underneath the white Honda Civic. She could hear the sound of metal on metal, a tight, solid frequency that sat heavily in her ears in a way she found uncomfortable but attractively decisive. She had an impulse to caress the webbing between Ást's toes, but she resisted, having already stayed too long.

"So, you're an Aquatic, right?" Ást asked from underneath the car, his voice disembodied from his feet.

"How can you tell?"

"It creates a certain appetite."

"Oh, it does not."

"What makes you risk being here?"

"My mother."

"She lives unwatered?"

"Yes."

"How old?"

"127."

"The *ryð*?"

"It runs early in the family."

"At?"

"Late 120s."

"Trying to get your blue light to shine, eh?" Ást said.

Even without being able to see her, Ást sensed that

he'd gone too far. Aquatics believe that those who, during their lifetime, reach *koma*, or sainthood, demonstrate their grace in two different ways, both of which happen when they die. The first is that they flash a brilliant blue light at the moment of their death. The second happens when their *upplifa* enters the clouds—they absorb not the characteristics of the cloud, but the cloud itself. The *koma upplifa* doesn't fall as rain, but uses the strength of the cloud to travel to the next world, the cloud disappearing with them.

"I'm sorry," Ást said. He remained underneath the white Honda Civic but stopped working on it. "I didn't mean to be mean."

"It's okay."

"But if she doesn't want to go back to the water?"

"It's not an option."

"You have a plan B, then."

"I do."

"You're willing to use force?"

"I guess I am."

Ást slid out from under the car. There was grease on his face, and his arms were thick in his T-shirt. "Everything's fine underneath," he said. "It should get you ... where again?"

"Morris. Manitoba."

"You'll be fine. That crack in the windshield's gonna keep growing, but you'll be fine."

"I really appreciate this. The water. Everything."

"You know, Aby, I'm a bit of an Aquatic as well."

"You can't be a bit of an Aquatic."

"Nonetheless, I know I'm following the *trú*, my *trú*," Ást said. He continued looking Aby in the eyes, even though all he found there was disbelief.

The Aquatic Bible contains many depictions of God, all of them contradictory. In the Book of Strays, God appears as a homely Síðri, uncouth and powerless. In the Book of Doubt, God appears as a turtle with two heads, each offering advice that contradicts the other. The Book of Endings fails to personify God at all, presenting the divine only as the deeds of all living things.

In total, the Aquatic Bible presents fourteen personifications of the divine, each having absolutely nothing to do with the others. In spite of this, or more probably because of it, the vast majority of Aquatics express their belief in God through the concept of the *trú*, which literally translates as "the current."

This is what the Síðri would call fate or destiny, although there is one key difference: *trú* carries no sense of predetermination. Aquatics believe it is possible—in fact, quite easy—to misplace your destiny. Losing the *trú* is as easy as losing your car keys. But following your *trú* is also easy, provided you submit to the current and let it take you where it wants you to be, regardless of your own desires.

"You think this is where your *trú* has taken you?" Aby said, unable to curb the disbelief in her voice.

"Yes."

"Unwatered?"

"I believe that to be the case."

"That's ... ah ... yeah."

"Your mother probably thinks so too," Ást said, and for the first time he looked away from Aby. "Something to think about, anyway."

Without giving her a chance to reply or washing his hands, Ást opened the door of the stolen white Honda Civic. Hesitating slightly, Aby got inside. As she began to work her legs around the steering wheel, Ást reached between them.

"What are you doing?"

"I'm moving the seat back."

"The seat moves back?" Aby said. It was so simple and obvious, but the possibility brought tears to her eyes.

"Here, get out," Ást said.

When the driver's seat was empty, Ást reached down and found the lever underneath it. He pulled up, and then slid the seat backwards. He showed Aby how to do this. She climbed back in. Holding the lever up, she slid back and forth repeatedly, laughing each time she did it.

Adjusting for maximum comfort, she looked up at Ást and slowly closed the driver's door. She wanted to thank him but feared she'd be misunderstood. So she didn't say anything. She kept the window rolled up and pressed her hand against it, spreading her fingers so the webbing became stretched and visible. Ást did the same. They held their hands like this for some time. Then Ást took a step back, leaving a greasy palm print on the glass.

17

Margaret's reasons

It was after one in the morning when Margaret, while climbing off the sailboat, saw two sets of headlights driving up the laneway to the Prairie Embassy Hotel. She stepped off the ladder and watched the cars park. Stewart had already started to dial Rebecca's number, but he closed his cellphone to watch. Each car held only the driver. Both were men. They got out of their vehicles and walked directly to the hotel.

"Who could that be?"

"The rainmakers," Margaret said. "I forgot all about them."

Putting the phone in his pocket, Stewart began climbing down the ladder, but Margaret waved him back. "No, no," she said. "Call her. She must really need you."

"Are you sure?"

"Yes."

"No, I mean, can you? Do you remember how to check someone in?"

"It's still my hotel."

"Okay. Okay," Stewart said.

Margaret watched him begin to dial, then turned and walked to the hotel. She was very sleepy—Stewart's cellphone had been ringing all night, keeping her up, but even a rested Margaret would have found the two men in her lobby odd. They stood so close together at the front desk that their elbows almost touched, but neither acknowledged the other's presence. One was slightly taller and younger, but in every other way they seemed extraordinarily similar—each was dressed in black from head to toe, carried a worn brown leather suitcase and had dark eyes and prominent cheekbones.

Margaret was so sleepy that she contemplated the possibility that they were the same person, the one on the right simply twenty years further into their shared lifespan. She moved to stand behind the front desk and looked at them again. This time she concluded that they were father and son, which explained both the resemblance and the lack of communication.

"Um, hi," Margaret said. "Can I help you?"

"The mayor's office said they'd arranged things," said the older one.

"I was told that the Morris Town Council had made reservations," said the younger.

"So you are the rainmakers?"

"Yes."

"I am."

"Yes, then, well, we'll have to get you registered," Margaret said.

It had been three years since Margaret had registered a

guest at the Prairie Embassy Hotel. However infrequently it needed to be done, the job was usually Stewart's. But figuring there couldn't be that much to it, Margaret began looking for the registry book. It took some minutes, as the desk was a mess. She had to search beneath inches of newspapers, half-open face-down books and rolls of nautical blueprints before she found it. She presented it to the men, each of whom reached into his breast pocket to pull out a pen. The younger one signed first, but he had to reach around the older one, who remained standing where he was. After both men had signed, Margaret turned the book around and read the names.

Anderson Richardson
Kenneth Richardson

Satisfied, Margaret closed the book. While it was good to have guests, all she really wanted was to get back to sleep, so she grabbed the first two keys that came to hand. The keys, which appeared to be antiques, were attached to flat lengths of wood. The room numbers were written in large block letters. Room #201 was handed to Anderson, while #202 went to Kenneth.

Looking around the lobby, both Anderson and Kenneth concluded that they might be the only guests at the Prairie Embassy Hotel. Yet the clerk had given them rooms right next to each other. They both wanted to complain, to request rooms on separate floors or at least on opposite ends of a floor, but that would mean acknowledging the other's presence, something neither man was prepared to do. Silently and simultaneously, both men nodded. They carried their own luggage as Margaret showed them to their rooms.

Two hours later, Margaret was once again woken from her sleep. She could hear Stewart hammering outside, but that wasn't what had woken her. It wasn't his cell phone either. She felt something trickling from her gills. The back of her head was wet, as were her shoulders. Margaret opened her eyes but did not move. She was scared to breathe. After several moments, as much out of need as from courage, Margaret opened her gills. When she pulled in air, her gills made a raspy, liquid sound and her darkest fears were confirmed.

Quickly and without looking behind her, Margaret got out of bed. She stood in front of the full-length mirror in the corner of her room. The floor was cold on the soles of her feet. Margaret wiggled her toes. These, she reluctantly observed, were not the toes of her youth. The realization made her sigh, which produced the raspy, liquid sound. Margaret looked up. Her neck was covered in a thick orange syrup. It dripped from her gills, momentarily collected at her collarbone, then slipped down between her breasts. Margaret could no longer deny it: the rust had begun.

As every Hliðafgoð knows, the *ryð* signals the beginning of the end. Some have lived for years after its appearance, others for only hours; most live for another few weeks. No cure has ever been found. Religious or not, each and every Hliðafgoð immediately begins the *bjarturvatn* as soon as the rust appears. *Bjarturvatn*, or "clear water," is the process of putting your financial, material and emotional houses in order. Since all Hliðafgoð are given such a concrete signal of their impending demise, it is considered intolerable to leave behind any unfinished business.

Financially, Margaret didn't have much to do. She supposed it would come to light that she didn't actually own the Prairie Embassy Hotel. The former proprietor had abandoned the building after two unsuccessful years of trying to sell it. Three years after that, Margaret had broken in through a second-storey window. After renovating the lobby and six of the thirty-eight rooms, she'd declared the Prairie Embassy Hotel open for business. In the seventeen years that followed, no one had seemed to notice that she didn't legally own the building, and Margaret had become an upstanding member of the community. Should the truth emerge, it wouldn't really affect anyone but Stewart. He would have to find a new place to work, but Margaret was sure this would be good for him. If anyone needed a fresh start, it was him.

Emotionally, Margaret felt settled as well. She had few close relationships in town. She should say some goodbyes, but they wouldn't be tearful. The only area that needed work was her relationship with her only child, Aberystwyth, whom she had not seen since leaving the water behind.

After graduating from an Aquatic seminary, Margaret had received her first parish in the farming community of Nowwlk. The congregation was small and had been dwindling for years. This was true of Aquatic congregations, both rural and urban, all across the country. So when Margaret's stern passion, direct approach and gift for words started bringing more and more Hliðafgoð into the Nowwlk parish, she quickly gathered attention.

But as her congregation grew, so did her doubts. While she continued to feel that Aquaticism offered truth, she had two major concerns. The first related to her amphibious nature. Margaret couldn't believe that God would have given her the ability to breathe air, equipping her body with such elegant biology, simply to forbid her from using it. The second was that, while she thought the Aquatic Bible held considerable insights into the Hliðafgoðian condition, she was unable to believe that anything within it had actually happened.

Meanwhile, her reputation as a preacher increased exponentially. Hliðafgoð were swimming for hours to hear her sermons. Nowwlk's only hotel had to be booked months in advance. Her acclaim grew so wide and so far that even the Aquatic Religious Council took note: they announced, with great fanfare, that the Augasteinn would visit the Nowwlk parish. While the more cynical dismissed it as little more than a media stunt, a way to bring attention to an Aquatic congregation that was growing instead of shrinking, no one could deny that it was a rare honour.

The morning of the Augasteinn's visit, the current had turned the water hot and murky. Margaret was nervous. She'd stayed up all night, tweaking the sermon the Council had already approved. Council representatives escorted her to the church and ushered her inside. The media presence was overwhelming. Cameras were everywhere. She counted sixteen microphones attached to the edge of the pulpit, with every major network represented. The Augasteinn and his people took up the first six rows, pushing her regular congregation to the back of the church.

Margaret looked over the crowd. She paused. She looked at the Augasteinn. She looked at the congregation. She knew that she would never have a moment like this again and she put her prepared sermon aside. She held up her copy of the Aquatic Bible. "This book is full of lies," she said.

It was not an auspicious beginning. The congregation collectively gasped.

"Beautiful, true, inspiring," Margaret continued. "But fiction. This book is filled with stories that can change your life, help you live, love, be loved. But these stories are not here to make us deny any part of ourselves. They are not here to bully us. The Bible teaches us that dying unwatered will curse your soul. How does that help us understand God? Or know God's love? It does not. It only keeps us in fear, leaving half of the grace God gave us unexplored and unused, something I feel God takes more as an insult than as a form of worship. Remember that the truth within yourself will always be greater than the truth found in these pages. These stories are here to guide us—to help us find that truth, not to tell us what it is."

By this time the Augasteinn had already reached the door. His people followed, and then so did her congregation. Margaret stood in front of the empty pews.

She was officially excommunicated the following day, by decree of the Augasteinn himself.

It was rumoured that Margaret left the water three days later, but that was not what really happened. It was hard for her to explain to those she loved, especially Aby, that her excommunication had not diminished her love of Aquaticism. It actually helped her find the confidence of her convictions. When, some eighteen months later, she did make the decision to live unwatered, she did not waver.

The only heartbreak came from leaving her daughter behind, something Margaret had not planned on doing. She had tried to bring Aby with her, but her daughter had refused to leave. But Margaret was sure that living unwatered was her *trú*. She knew that resisting it would only cause her futile pain and sorrow. So while she found it difficult to put her religious convictions ahead of her love for her daughter, she believed it was God's will. She was sure God would convince Aby to join her at some future time. She did not expect this to take more than two or three years.

Standing in front of the full-length mirror, with the rust trailing orange lines down her green skin, Margaret decided that her *bjarturvatn* need not include any reconciliation with her daughter. She would spend no more of her now finite time and energy thinking about it. Margaret stood in front of the mirror for many more minutes, watching as more and more rust seeped from her gills. She tried to convince herself that her decision was for the best, but failed miserably.

18

One great city!

Aby was tired, still more than three hours outside of
Winnipeg, and had no words to describe the horrible
feeling in her legs. It was as if a thousand tiny, jagged
pieces of shell were floating through her bloodstream,
pushing at her skin from the inside. Aby had vowed
that she would not stop until she was on the far side of
Winnipeg, but as the sensation grew severe, she had to.
Slowing down, Aby pulled onto the side of the road. She
got out of the white Honda Civic, attempted to take a
step and collapsed. Leaning on the hood, she looked at
the long crack in the windshield.

Even though Ást had told her she didn't have to worry
about the crack in the windshield, Aby did. But as the
kilometres went by, she'd managed to turn her worry into
a game: if she reached the Prairie Embassy Hotel before
the crack touched the left-hand corner of the windshield,
her mother would still be alive. The rust would not
have started. In addition, both more importantly and
more improbably, Margaret would be receptive to her

daughter's unannounced visit. As Aby drove through Manitoba, most of her understood that this was simply a way to make the time pass more quickly, but a small part of her began to believe it. Now the crack was less than two inches from the corner of the windshield.

Aby stood at the side of the Trans-Canada Highway, alarmed by the continuing and still unnamed sensation in her legs. She feared it was permanent, but after five minutes of leaning against the stolen white Honda Civic, she began to feel better. After fifteen minutes, the sensation was gone. Determined to get past Winnipeg, if not all the way to Morris, before she slept, Aby got back into the driver's seat.

Three and a half hours later, Aby reached the outskirts of Winnipeg. The sky was moonless, the road was not well marked and Aby was tired. All of this led to confusion, and instead of bypassing the city, Aby found herself in the centre of it. Her attempts to return to the highway only led her to residential streets. Just after 10:00 p.m., her eyes were beginning to close on their own, and Aby acknowledged that she needed to rest. She selected a quiet, tree-lined street and after several attempts managed to parallel park. She reclined her seat and fell asleep quickly.

A short time later Aby was startled awake when she heard someone at her right rear tire. Eagerness to get out of Winnipeg made her forget her promise to have as little contact with the Síðri as possible. She opened the car door, stepped onto the pavement and walked to the rear of the vehicle. At first she thought she had hit the young man who was squatting on the curb, because his body was so close to the back bumper. But he appeared uninjured, so Aby relaxed, though just slightly.

"Mavbe vou could velph me?" she asked.

The man did not immediately respond, which made Aby very nervous. Her gills opened and closed slightly and she wiggled her fingers, stretching the webbing between them. Aby was unaware that she was doing this until the Síðri looked at his hands. Self-conscious, Aby put hers behind her back.

Finally, after what seemed like a very long time, he spoke. "I think I know you," he said.

"I von't fink sooh."

"Yeah, I do. You almost crashed into a limousine I was in."

"Fat was vou?" He looked very different.

"I was in the back."

"Neye am so soohrry aboot vat," Aby said. "Please vait here?"

The man continued to squat, and Aby took his lack of movement as agreement. Still impressed with her improving ability to walk, Aby returned to the car and thrust her head into the back seat. She knew she'd hidden the keys somewhere safe, but she suddenly couldn't remember where that was. After pushing her hand down the crack in the seat behind the seat belts, then searching in the pocket in the driver's side door, she found them underneath the back floor mats. Holding them firmly, Aby returned to the man, who had remained at the back of the car.

"Cav vou please make saue fese get back tau her?"

Aby asked. She held out her hand. At first it seemed like the man would deny her request. Then, slowly, he reached out his hand. Careful to make her movements slow and predictable, so as not to spook him, she handed over the keys.

"I will," he said. He stared at the keys.

"Verv impaurtant."

"It's unbelievable," the man said.

His answer satisfied Aby, as she assumed he'd meant it in the Aquatic sense of the word. Returning the keys was a weight off her shoulders and filled her with satisfaction and renewed energy. "Dou vou phow vow to get to Morris?" she asked him.

"Where?

"Vit's verv close. Morris?"

"Sorry. I'm not from around here."

"Auh. Auvay. Feranks, then."

"No problem."

"It's sau drv here."

"I find that too," he said.

Aby nodded. The man returned the gesture. She felt that this brief interaction had somehow been significant, of even greater significance than returning the keys. Perhaps he was an *Almennt*, a word that has no English translation, but that describes God's brief appearance in the world in exactly the form the seer needs to see.

Aby looked back at the man to see if this was true, but he just continued to stand there, looking dumbfounded, and she concluded that he wasn't an *Almennt*. She got back inside the white Honda Civic, rolled up the window and started the engine. The gills in her neck opened and she took a very deep breath, then mistakenly put the car into reverse. Still feeling like something had been left unsaid, Aby gave a small, embarrassed wave, then pulled onto the street. She was less than two hours away from Morris, but first she'd have to find her way out of Winnipeg using nothing but *allt*, or, in English, trial and error.

19

The Richardsons

Kenneth Richardson had begun rainmaking in 1978, at the age of twenty-two. He'd had no one to teach him but had stumbled onto a process of filling small cloth bags with silver iodide and attaching the bags to a flock of starlings he tamed and trained himself. The birds, sixty or seventy at a time, would fly into a cloud. The silver iodide would fall out through tiny holes he'd cut in the cloth. The cloud would be seeded, and rain would begin to fall roughly five minutes later. Kenneth was never sure how it worked. He just knew it did.

After becoming quite successful as a rainmaker, Kenneth got married in 1980 and had a son, whom they named Anderson, the following year. When Anderson turned fourteen, Kenneth's business became Richardson & Son, and they took the rainmaking world by storm. Seven wonderful years passed. They were the best there ever was, turning water-starved fields into bumper crops, saving livestock and livelihoods.

But then, in 2002, Anderson had an idea. He put

seven car batteries in a circle, attached copper wire to the positive and negative poles, and raised the wires until they met at a point five feet in the air. Next, he built a kite, which he flew on a copper wire. When the kite was in the clouds, Anderson attached the batteries. An electric current climbed up the copper string and into the clouds. There was a flash, then thunder, and then rain began to fall.

Anderson recreated his experiment for his father, expecting approval. He did not get it. Kenneth found the use of electricity crass. The kite was lazy and undisciplined. They fought, and from that day forward they never spoke again. Through written correspondence, they divided the country: Kenneth took jobs in the western states and Anderson in the east. Canada had never been discussed, never even considered. When they got the calls to come to Morris, each man assumed the territory was his.

It was because of this rivalry that, the morning after they'd checked in, Kenneth and Anderson Richardson left the Prairie Embassy Hotel in different cars. They drove into downtown Morris and began searching for very different, yet very specific items. It did not take Kenneth long to discover Snyder's Photography Studio, where he purchased the entire stock of silver iodide. Anderson's search began and ended at Nixon's Auto Wreckers, where he bought five used car batteries. Both men then drove back to the hotel and carried their purchases up to the roof.

Just before noon on August 25th, Kenneth and Anderson occupied different corners on the roof of the

Prairie Embassy Hotel. Anderson took the northeast corner and began placing more car batteries than he'd ever used before in a circle. Kenneth, in the southwest corner, carefully added as much powder to each of his pouches as he dared. Then they sat on the roof, waiting for the perfect cloud to appear.

20

234.7 metres above sea level

Aberystwyth's foot continued to depress the left pedal as the white Honda Civic idled at the top of the laneway. Her gills widened. She breathed, lifted her foot and then pressed too hard on the gas. The white Honda Civic began fishtailing in the gravel. Aby oversteered and the car began travelling sideways. Returning her foot to the brake, Aby turned her head to the right and watched through the passenger window as the Prairie Embassy Hotel quickly approached. Her grip on the steering wheel became tighter. The car stopped of its own accord, two feet from the porch.

Dust curled in the driver's side window and settled on Aby's fingers, which continued holding the steering wheel. Her knuckles were the only part of her that was pale. The rest of her had become an iridescent dark forest green. The brake remained pressed against the all-weather floor mats, and the engine continued to run. Aby stayed in this position for several minutes, until her right leg began to tremble. Relaxing her grip on the steering wheel,

Aby lifted her foot from the pedal. The gills in her neck flapped open and she took a deep breath. The dust made her cough. Reaching up, Aby traced the length of the crack in the windshield with her index finger and stopped where the crack did, half an inch from the top left corner. Aby had won. Her gills pulled in and pushed out an especially large volume of air. Beating the crack filled her with a gust of optimism, although this was tempered when the dust made her cough a second time.

She shifted in the driver's seat so that she could see all five storeys of the Prairie Embassy Hotel below the crack. Aby feared the building was abandoned, although all Síðri buildings looked unoccupied to her. It was certainly much smaller than she'd expected. The wood looked flimsy. She didn't like its faded yellow colour, and she didn't like that it had held her mother for so many years.

Aby shut off the motor but remained inside the car, keeping her finger on the far end of the crack. When her hand started cramping, Aby stretched her fingers in front of her face and massaged the webbing between them. She leaned back in her seat and closed her eyes. Moments later, she became convinced that she was being watched. Opening her eyes, she saw her mother staring through the driver's side window. Aby smiled, but her smile was not returned.

Margaret did not blink, and her face revealed no emotion of any kind. "I'm not going back," Margaret said.

Aby rolled down her window.

"I'm not going back," Margaret repeated.

"That's not why I'm here."

"Are you still Aquatic?"

"Let's not start there," Aby said, but Margaret had already turned and was walking away from the car.

Aby opened the car door. She had some difficulty getting out of the driver's seat, but bolstered by her recent success with walking and running, she didn't fear the uneven ground. She put all her weight on her left foot, and then, hoping to at least appear casual, she took a step. She did not fall. She took another, then another. When she looked up to see her mother's reaction, an apple struck her firmly on the chest.

Waving her arms to remain upright, Aby looked in the direction the apple had come from and saw her mother standing on the porch of the Prairie Embassy Hotel. There was a second apple in her hand and a basket of them at her feet. "I will not go back!" Margaret yelled. She aimed, and threw.

Aby ducked the second apple, but the third hit her squarely on her forehead, knocking her off balance. The fourth apple grazed Aby's nose as she fell backwards. As she tried to get to her feet, apples struck her shoulders, and others landed inches from her head. On her hands and knees, Aby craled to the white Honda Civic. Apples hit the hood of the car, producing metallic thuds. Two apples struck the windshield as she got in and closed the door. Sitting behind the wheel, Aby watched an apple strike the exact centre of the windshield, causing the crack to reach the top left corner.

PART SIX

The Impostors

Lewis II

21

The clumsy hand of God

Lewis stood up and then sat back down on the bench. Quickly, without giving himself time to lose his nerve, he stood up again and walked across the street. He took his hands out of his pockets, opened the door of Ear Candy Records and stepped inside. The brown carpet needed vacuuming. A thin man wearing a green T-shirt and black jeans stood behind the counter, reading a magazine. He had the same hairstyle Lewis had had before his haircut in Winnipeg.

Lewis stood in front of the New Releases section, searching for a CD. It wasn't there. He walked to the bins and flipped through the I's from first to last. It wasn't there, either. Putting his hands back in his pockets, Lewis reluctantly walked to the front counter, where the clerk continued reading.

"Um," Lewis said. "There's a record I can't seem to find."

"Yeah?" the clerk said. He put his index finger on the

place where he'd been reading and scratched his scruffy beard.

"The Impostors?"

The clerk looked at Lewis. Lewis watched for signs of recognition, but none appeared: a haircut and a change of clothes had been all he'd needed as a disguise. This made Lewis feel both very safe and very sad.

The clerk gave a tiny, dismissive laugh, then lifted his finger and returned to his magazine. "Try the mall," he said, flipping the page.

"Excuse me?"

"We don't have it."

"You sound proud."

"I am."

"Why?"

The clerk looked up, closed his magazine and folded his hands on top of it. He leaned slightly forward. "Because it's not really music," he said. "It's product."

"It's in the top five!"

"Exactly."

"All over the world."

"Hey, listen. I don't want to come off as a snob," the clerk said, raising his hands open-palmed in the air. "You can listen to whatever you want. But I mean, that band's a one-hit wonder, and it's already over. If you want some pop music, that's fine, that's great, but why don't you try some Abba? Or the Beach Boys? Maybe the Cars? Greatest hits, anyway. Really, I can show you some great stuff."

"Can you show a little more respect?"

"Hey, wait, I mean—"

"You know she's dead?"

"Yeah, I heard that. Weird, eh?"

"You should be sorry," Lewis yelled. "You should be very, very sorry!"

Lewis was suddenly unable to stop yelling. Every part of his body seemed to be yelling. His fists were yelling, his ears were yelling. His feet yelled at the floor as he walked across it, pushed the door open and left.

$\approx$

Lewis would never have met his wife if he hadn't let his sister cut his hair during Christmas break of grade twelve. As with most siblings, Lewis's relationship with his sister had involved a strange mixture of envy, hostility and loyalty. But when Joanne moved to Vancouver to take a job cutting hair at a friend's salon, Lewis was surprised to discover that he missed her. He was even more surprised to learn that Joanne missed him too. When she came home for the holidays, they stayed up together, drinking rum and eggnog and watching the Christmas specials they'd formerly squabbled in front of. Nostalgia seeped into everything, and on Christmas Eve, after their parents had gone to bed, Joanne asked if she could cut his hair.

Lewis didn't see how he could say no. Joanne tied a towel around his neck as he sat on a chair in the kitchen. She did not ask how he wanted his hair to be cut, she simply started. Bits of hair fell between the towel and his skin, and because of this Lewis would associate an itchy neck with transformation for the rest of his life.

She would not let him see the work in progress. Finally, with a great flourish, she removed the towel. Lewis ran upstairs. He locked the bathroom door. He closed his eyes. He moved in front of the mirror, took a very deep breath and, very slowly, opened his eyes. Joanne had cut his hair in a style Lewis would never have selected for himself. It was fashionable and hip. It was everything he wasn't and everything he wanted to be. He ran downstairs and told her, without the irony that seasoned so many of their conversations, that it was the best Christmas present he'd ever had. Which was good, as it was the only one Joanne had for him.

The following Monday, the hostility Lewis received from the boys at school was more than compensated for by the attention he got from the girls. Donna Walter, who had previously ignored him completely even though her locker was right next to his, spent the time between third and fourth period talking to him. When the bell rang, she didn't move, so Lewis didn't either. The hallway filled with students. Donna continued to look at him. He continued to lean against his locker. The hallway emptied, and the bell for fourth period rang.

"Don't you have class?" she asked.

"Sheet-Metal Welding."

Donna took two steps backwards, turned and walked away. Lewis waited and was rewarded when Donna looked over her shoulder four steps later, smiling. Lewis returned her smile, briefly, then began walking to Sheet-Metal Welding. Compared with his first successful flirtation, being five minutes late for shop class didn't seem like a big deal. The only downside was that, by the time he arrived, everyone already had a partner and the only empty seat was next to Lisa Reynolds.

Lisa Reynolds was unpopular. Her hair was black, shoulder-length and lank at a time when everyone else's was short, shiny and blond. She wore T-shirts for bands that only fathers had heard of. She seemed to smile all the time, and her teeth had gaps and were crooked. She didn't carry books, binders or a pencil case, but any time a teacher asked her a question she knew the answer, and this, above all else, made her uncool. But even worse than any of those transgressions was that Lisa Reynolds took shop. In a school of close to a thousand students, she was the only girl who did so.

Lewis sat down beside her. Lisa waited for him to introduce himself. She waited in vain. No words passed between them. The end of the period was nearing when Lisa said the only thing that could possibly have made Lewis give her his full attention. She was not flattering him. She was not being manipulative. She simply said exactly what was on her mind, as was her habit.

"We should start a band," she said. "You could be the lead singer."

Throughout the rest of the semester, very little sheet-metal welding got done. Lewis and Lisa used fourth period to fabricate their band instead. They didn't buy instruments or take music lessons. Instead, they concentrated on what the band's name would be and what they would look like onstage. From January 7 to January 10 they both liked the name The Stranger Things. The

Stranger Things was envisioned as a large band, with an all-male horn section wearing identical brown tuxedos with baby blue ruffled shirts. There would be female backup singers dressed in tight knee-length skirts and white silk blouses. They'd play soul music, but there would also be two synthesizer players with new-wave haircuts to give the band a contemporary edge.

Then Lisa spent a Sunday afternoon skimming her sister Rebecca's Greek Mythology textbook, and the band's name was changed to Myth of Sisyphus. In this band, Lisa would stand mid-stage in a blue spotlight, singing nonsensical lyrics. Three cello players dressed in formal wear would play to her right. Lewis would wander across the stage, playing different musical instruments, such as guitar, banjo, xylophone and toy piano.

The following week they became Unwashed Teen Punk Band, soon shortened to Teen Punk Band. This marked a significant and irreversible evolution. As a punk band, they would not require musical talent—they had invented a band they could actually form. Although the name changed daily, the band remained a punk band for the next several weeks. By the middle of February, they were on the verge of buying guitars when Lisa admitted that she didn't really want to be in a punk band. Lewis conceded that he had no desire to be in one either. Neither really felt that angry.

For seventeen days their band had no name. The dream began to fade, and Lisa and Lewis felt themselves drifting apart. Forming a band was downgraded from goal to aspiration to idea. Then Lisa purchased a Casio keyboard from a second-hand shop for seventeen dollars. By repeatedly complimenting him on his voice, she persuaded Lewis that this was all they needed.

They rehearsed in Lisa's basement for three weeks. Since they couldn't read music or play by ear, Lewis and Lisa decided to write a song instead of learning someone else's. They called it "Sounds Like Something Forever." It featured a very simple keyboard melody, and the lyrics, written by Lisa, told the story of best friends who discover true love in each other. On the last day of school before March break, at the final assembly Battle of the Bands, Lewis and Lisa performed their first gig.

They waited stage left as Threats of Youth, which Lisa and Lewis agreed was a fantastic name, finished to wild applause. Lewis and Lisa walked onstage. Lisa carried her Casio under her arm. Lewis had only his voice and his haircut. Lisa plugged in. Lewis looked at his feet, and they began to play.

Lewis was never able to remember details about the performance. He couldn't remember how he sang, although he assumed poorly. He couldn't remember how well Lisa played, although he believed badly, considering her instrument was a Casio keyboard. But what was clear in his mind was how, just after the second chorus and as the bridge began, he'd dared to look up, out into the audience, and was instantly transformed. All his life Lewis had felt alienated, separated and removed. During the performance, these feelings remained, but onstage the usual dynamic was inverted. He wasn't being cast out but elevated. He didn't feel rejected but acclaimed. He never wanted it to end.

There was little applause. They did not win the competition. But two days later they decided to move to Halifax and study at the Nova Scotia College of Art and Design. It was a decision that seemed to arrive premade with the course calendar and application forms. Neither Lisa nor Lewis had been to the east coast of Canada. They'd never lived away from their parents. They still hadn't kissed. But they both applied and were accepted, and neither questioned this.

Three weeks before classes started, they arrived in Halifax, carrying one backpack each. They stayed at the Halifax International Hostel on the south end of Barrington Street. The hostel had a strict policy: un-married men and women had to sleep in separate rooms. So every night Lisa would make sure she got a bottom bunk, which Lewis would sneak into shortly after three. They would hold each other for the rest of the night and then, just before sunrise, Lewis would return to his room.

Nine nights later they found a two-bedroom apartment on the fourth floor of a rundown building at the corner of Creighton and Cornwallis. The building swayed when the breeze was strong, but if Lisa stood on a chair in the corner of her room she had a harbour view. Every night Lewis would go to bed on his futon, crawl into Lisa's bed an hour later and then return to his room just before the sun rose.

When school started, Lewis and Lisa began studying

how to become artists. Since they couldn't be sure whether they were artists or not, they mimicked those who were. They drank. They smoked constantly. They hung out in dive bars. Shortly after Christmas break, they started sleeping around. Or at least, Lisa did. Lewis, despite initial opportunities and enthusiasm, tired of it quickly.

At first, Lewis tried to ignore the late-night noises coming from Lisa's side of the wall. When that failed, he tried to make art out of it. He took photos of the different shoes he found at the back door of his apartment. He created sculptures with the different brands of cigarettes left in the ashtray. He signed out microphones and tape decks from the AV department and made field recordings in the middle of the night.

Then one night Lewis put the pillow over his head, a blanket over the pillow and his hands over the blanket, but he still heard everything. When it was over, Lewis listened to the footsteps leaving Lisa's room. These footsteps were heavy. They were not Lisa's. Hearing the bathroom door close, Lewis opened the door of his bedroom. In three steps he was in front of Lisa's door. He opened it. He stood, motionless and backlit from the light in the kitchen.

"Lewis?"

He did not reply. He stepped into her bedroom and onto her futon and pulled off the comforter. He stooped and gathered her up. Lisa did not speak or resist. She remained silent even as Lewis, with a bend of his knees, swung her over his shoulder and carried her out of the room. Lewis shut the door of his bedroom with his foot.

He tossed Lisa onto his bed. He held the covers over their heads as the bathroom door opened.

"Lisa?" they heard the guy with the heavy footsteps whisper. "Lisa?"

They listened to him in her bedroom. They listened to him walk through the kitchen. They listened to him check the other rooms of the apartment. They listened to him put on his shoes and leave. When he had gone, Lewis said, "I'm jealous."

"Finally."

"Will you marry me?"

"Absolutely."

That night they went all the way.

They were married, albeit in a civil ceremony, nineteen months later. After the wedding, Lisa and Lewis began working collaboratively. Four years later, for their thesis project, they decided to create a band. Not just start a band but create one, fully formed, as if it had sprung from their foreheads. They decided on the name: The Impostors. They created a logo. They silk-screened it onto T-shirts, then hung them in second-hand clothing stores. Posters for gigs never played were designed, printed, aged in the oven and stapled underneath older posters around town. Using Lisa's Casio, they recorded a secret demo, which they burned onto CDs, labelled *The Impostors—Demo*. The CDs were left on buses and in coffee shops. They created a web page disguised as a fan site and leaked the demo to the Internet.

They received a passing grade for blurring the line between fiction and fact. The line was blurred even further three weeks later when Steven Tassle, then head of acquisitions at Broken Records, loved the demo, simply had to have it and personally flew to Halifax to sign the band. The only stipulation was that they re-record "Sounds Like Something Forever" to be released as the first single.

Lewis did not realize how large a scene he had made until he was safely across the street and sitting once again on the bench. The record store clerk was looking at him through the front window of the store. Scratching his scruffy beard, the clerk talked on his cellphone, no doubt describing the customer who had lost it over a has-been pop band. Lewis's palms were still wet. His heartbeat remained quick. He twisted his legs to the left so he wouldn't be facing the record store, and this afforded him a view of a basketball court attached to a public school. There was only one person on the court, and it was Lisa.

Her dirty, straggly hair was pulled into a ponytail that seemed to sprout from the top of her head. After she jumped but before her feet landed on the ground, the ponytail stood completely upright, making her head look like the dot of an exclamation mark. She was dressed in a ripped greyish-white T-shirt, although there was no mustard stain over her nipple today.

Lewis watched as she practised her jump shot. In the time he sat on the bench, Lisa made seven rushes towards the hoop, none of which succeeded. On her eighth pass, she dribbled on the toe of her left foot and ended up kicking the ball to the far end of the court. This made Lewis laugh. His laughter caught Lisa's attention. After retrieving the ball, she stood at the far end of the court and faced him, turning the orange basketball slowly in her hands.

Lewis lifted his right hand slightly, giving a small wave.

"Wanna play?" Lisa asked.

"Sure," Lewis said. He got off the bench. He jogged around the fence and onto the court. He held out his hands to receive the ball.

"Let's just start with twenty-one," Lisa said. She passed Lewis the ball, and he moved to stand at the foul line.

"Who said you could start?" she asked.

"I just assumed."

"Well, don't."

"You start, then."

"Definitely," Lisa said. She stood at the foul line with her toes slightly over it. She dribbled the ball three times. She held it tightly with both hands. She raised it. A look of intense concentration came over her face, and then she took her shot. The ball sailed through the air and over the backboard, landing in the grass on the other side.

Lewis laughed.

"What?"

"Nothing. I'll get it."

Jogging, Lewis retrieved the basketball. He passed it back to Lisa. Again, she dribbled the ball. She raised it high. She shot. The ball sailed over the backboard without touching it.

Lewis laughed again.

"What?"

"I just thought ... you know."

"What?"

"I thought God might be a little better at shooting hoops," Lewis said. Lisa glared at him, but Lewis was unable to eliminate the smile from his face. "I'll give you a ten-point lead if you answer one simple question."

"Shoot."

"Where do we go when we die?"

"Go get the ball," Lisa said, setting her hands on her hips. Lewis nodded and ran to the grass, returning with the ball. He passed it to her and Lisa dribbled it three times. "I have no idea," she said. "I haven't died, and I never will. Mortality is your thing, not mine." Raising the ball, Lisa shot. The ball hit the rim and bounced back onto the grass.

"I'm not fetching it this time," Lewis said.

Without protest, Lisa retrieved the basketball. She bounce-passed it to Lewis, who stood at the edge of the foul line. He raised the ball and shot. The ball sailed through the hoop.

Lisa chased it, and passed it to Lewis, who had not moved from the foul line. Lewis aimed. He shot. The ball went through the hoop again.

Lisa retrieved it. Lewis shot again. Again he scored. His next shot was also a winner, but the one that followed circled the rim and bounced out of the hoop. Lisa was quick to the rebound, retrieving the ball directly to the left of the basket. She raised it. She aimed. She brought the ball back down and held it against her hip. "I'll tell you what," she said. She leaned over to tie her right shoelace. Her shirt hung open, revealing her braless breasts. "If I make this shot, I win the game."

"Why would I agree to that?"

"Because if I lose, I'll tell you the meaning of life."

"Lisa, I don't really believe that you're God."

"That's okay. I don't really believe you're a rock star."

"Alright, then," Lewis said. "Shoot."

Lisa turned the ball slightly in her fingers. She raised it. She shot. The ball sailed through the air, missing both hoop and backboard completely. Together they watched the ball land on the grass, and then Lewis looked at Lisa expectantly.

"You idiot," she said. "There is no meaning. There's no plan. No script. It's not a movie. There's no lasting significance. No great reward. No right. No wrong. No punishment. No justice. There's no heaven or hell. Forget all that. There's no reason for any of this. It's all random. Everything's fucking random!"

She stopped. She caught her breath. She continued. "You can invent something. You can make up some sort of meaning. You can make the boy get the girl. You can tie up the loose ends. You can persuade yourself that suffering brings redemption." With these words she paused. She looked directly into Lewis's eyes, extending her index finger. She took a step towards him, invading his personal space. "But you know what?" She touched his chest with her finger. "You know the one thing I do know? All that suffering brings is bitterness. Eventually, no matter who you are, no matter how firmly you believe in heaven, or karma, or the way, it all ends with bitterness. None of those things can protect you. Tell me that seventy years of anything, of happiness, of euphoria, is worth seven months of bowel cancer. You can't. It isn't."

Lewis attempted to form a reply, but Lisa turned her back. She dropped her basketball and walked off the court, leaving Lewis alone.

22

The ghosts in the Vice-Regal Suite

It was just before midnight when Lewis began to search his hotel suite for the basketball. He was sure he'd brought it with him. He remembered picking it up from the pavement of the basketball court. He remembered dribbling it along Broadway Avenue and up the steps of the Fort Garry Hotel. He remembered tucking it under his arm to carry it across the lobby. He was sure he'd bounced it against the wall of the elevator, accidentally requesting floors seven, eight and eleven. But now he couldn't find it anywhere. He searched the bathroom, the living room, under the bed and behind the television. But he couldn't remember what he'd done with it.

At midnight, Lewis undressed, climbed into bed and pulled up the covers. At 12:17, he turned the clock to face the wall. He fluffed his pillow. He turned on his side and curled up into a little ball. Still he could not stop thinking about the basketball.

Shortly after two o'clock, Lewis got up, dressed and

left the Vice-Regal Suite. He walked the length of the hallway. He did not find his basketball. He walked up and down every hallway on his floor, but still, no basketball. He pressed the down button for the elevator and waited. When the right-hand one arrived, Lewis let it leave without him. He pressed the down button again. When the left-one one arrived, he got in, as this was the one he'd come up in, but there was no basketball inside it.

Lewis went down. The doors opened in the lobby. He walked to the front desk. He was glad that the clerk named Beth was working and that she was alone.

"Good evening," Beth said.

"Do you have a lost and found?"

"We do."

"Do you have a basketball in it?"

"I'll have to check," she said, but she did not move. She seemed to be waiting for some sign from Lewis.

"I'll wait," Lewis said. Looking over her shoulder, Beth went through the door behind the desk. Lewis waited. He was the only one in the lobby. There were no guests. No concierge. Lewis was alone in a room designed to hold hundreds, and for a moment he became frightened that, with no one watching him, he might begin to disappear forever. Then he heard Beth come through the door and return to her station behind the desk.

"Sorry. No basketball. No sports equipment of any kind."

"Oh," Lewis said. This saddened him.

"Are you okay?"

"I'm just fine. Really fine. I just can't seem to find my basketball."

Lewis turned towards the elevator and did not see that the look of concern remained on Beth's face. He did not look back while he waited for the elevator. He rode it directly to his floor. He went straight to his room, unlocked the door with his pass card and was surprised to find his wife standing just to the left of the bed. She was full-sized, but transparent.

"Quickly," she told him. "I can't hold this for long."

"I'm so sorry."

"You're so messed up right now."

"I know."

"You have to deal with it."

"You want me to grieve faster?"

"Lewis, you haven't even started."

Lewis stepped into the room, closing the door behind him. His wife had already begun to fade. He could see the carpet through her legs and the floral print wallpaper behind her shoulders and head.

"What should I do?"

"For starters, you have to stop listening to that woman."

"I know. I know. She's no good."

"But you're doing the right thing."

"What thing? What am I doing?"

"Just keep doing it."

"What? What am I doing?"

"Just keep making it tactile. Making it something you can touch . . ."

There was more, but it was too quiet for Lewis to hear. With a small but audible poof, she disappeared.

23

Some semblance of order

Lewis sat on the edge of the bed and, although he tried not to, began to cry. After three deep sobs and four deeper breaths, Lewis went into the bathroom, where he wiped his nose and tried to figure out how to make things tactile. He asked himself what he felt inside. He told himself to stop thinking, stop talking and became perfectly still. When he did, he remembered a winter night seventeen months after they'd married, when they were still in Halifax and in their fourth year of art school.

For six weeks they'd been arguing, although he was unable to remember what the fight was about. All he knew was that he'd decided to leave, but Lisa had convinced him to spend one last night. They slept together one last time, and it was so boisterous and gymnastic that Lewis fell asleep immediately afterwards. While he slept, Lisa took a steak knife, went outside and slashed all four tires of his car.

In the morning, Lewis was carrying a box filled with his most precious possessions when he noticed that all his tires were flat.

Furious, Lewis stormed back into their apartment, accusing her in the kitchen. She did not deny it. His initial reaction was that she was crazy, and it validated his decision to leave. But he soon reinterpreted the gesture as a sincere display of affection. On the condition that she paid for the new tires, and that she do so before the end of the week, he decided to stay.

It was only now, standing in the bathroom of the second-best hotel room in Winnipeg, Manitoba, that Lewis realized how much more her actions had meant. At that moment, when the honeymoon glow had completely faded, when he was exhausted from the fighting and disheartened by the wet Halifax winter, he would have left her. Had Lewis been able to drive away, he would done so, and he wouldn't have looked back until it was impossible to return. With four simple thrusts of a kitchen knife, Lisa had made this impossible, saving not only their relationship, but him.

Lewis looked up from the bathroom floor at his reflection. He couldn't believe he'd made her pay for the tires. "There," he said to himself. "That's a great example of you being an asshole." He walked out to the living room, where he plucked the steak knife from the dishes he had yet to set in the hall and left the suite.

It was in the elevator, descending, that Lewis crystallized the plan: he would deflate all four tires of a car. If that didn't make things tactile enough, he would deflate all the tires on another car. He was prepared to stick his steak knife into as many tires as it took. However—and this was very important to him—the destruction couldn't be completely random: whether they were all hatchbacks, or all had headlights that folded down, or all had out-of-province licence plates, the cars needed to be somehow related. Lewis wanted destruction, but it had to have a structure, a guiding principle, some semblance of order.

Lewis walked through the lobby and nodded to Beth. He was three streets north of the hotel when he decided the theme would be cracks in the windshield, primarily because he was passing a BMW that had a long horizontal crack in its windshield. Lewis knelt down at the right back tire of the car. He put his hand on the bumper, which felt very cold. He pulled the knife out of the inside pocket of his jacket and, with considerable effort, pushed it into the tire.

Doing this made Lewis feel very happy. He listened to the air escaping and pushed the knife up and down so it exited faster. When the tire had visibly flattened, Lewis tried to pull out the knife. The knife resisted. Only after several attempts did Lewis succeed in removing it. Keeping the knife in his hand, Lewis circled the BMW, slashing each tire as he passed it. He stood in the middle of the street, turning the steak knife in his hand. He watched as the other three tires deflated, and then began to search for another car with a crack in the windshield.

Winnipeg was a Prairie town, surrounded by gravel roads and farms, and Lewis had anticipated that cars with cracked windshields would be common. But after searching for forty-five minutes, he hadn't found another one. Lewis was about to change the theme when he turned right onto Wolseley Street and his eyes focused on a white Honda Civic. Even from half a block away he could see the crack that started in the middle of the windshield and travelled upwards towards the left-hand corner. Lewis ran towards the car, then crouched at the back right tire. He pulled the steak knife out of his pocket. He heard the driver's door open and became very still.

Lewis had assumed the car was unoccupied but had not checked. His mind reviewed his options. They seemed limited. He was still trying to decide what to do when he saw a green foot step onto the pavement. The right foot, which was also green, soon followed it. Both feet were webbed and began walking towards him. Continuing to squat, Lewis set the knife on the ground and looked up. A green-skinned woman with gills in her neck looked down. Lewis recognized her immediately.

Lewis could not believe he was staring at the same creature that had nearly T-boned their limo in Toronto. He looked from her hands to his—that his were neither green nor webbed seemed somehow inappropriate.

"Mavbe vou could velph me?" it asked.

"I think I know you," Lewis said.

"I von't fink sooh."

"Yeah, I do. You almost crashed into a limousine I was in."

"Fat was vou?"

"I was in the back."

"Neye am so soohrry aboot vat," Aby said. "Please vait here?"

Nodding, Lewis watched her walk awkwardly away.

When she returned, she held out her right hand. He was scared to touch her, not because he was repulsed, or afraid of her green skin (which did look a bit slimy), but because he knew that once he touched her the reality of her existence would become forever undeniable. After some moments, Lewis reached out his arm. Her skin felt cool and dry. She handed him a set of keys.

Lewis did not recognize them until he turned them over. There, on the back of the E.Z. Self Storage key chain, was a picture of Lisa, no older than twelve, with her family. Although Lewis was having trouble absorbing it, there was no denying that a green-skinned woman in the middle of a city he'd never been to before had just handed him a picture of his dead wife.

"Cav vou please make saue fese get back tau her?"

"I will."

"Verv impaurtant."

"It's unbelievable."

After she drove away, Lewis, still stunned, looked down and saw the steak knife on the pavement. The blade was slightly bent from where the Honda had driven over it. Keeping the keys firmly grasped in his right and, Lewis picked up the knife with his left and tucked it between his belt and his pants. He sat on the curb for several minutes. On his way back to the hotel, he slipped the knife between grates in the sewer.

PART SEVEN

Repressing Nothing

Rebecca III

24

David Sharpen

At 6:05 a.m. the day after throwing all things Stewart into the Dumpster, Rebecca sat in the unpopulated lab, composing a list of all the tasks she had postponed since the death of her sister. When finished, the list had seventeen items that needed her immediate attention. She had three of them accomplished before the majority of her co-workers arrived. By noon, she'd completed twelve. At 3:15 p.m., she drew a line across cross-hatchings, the last item on her list.

Sitting at her desk, Rebecca spun clockwise in her chair. She released a large, satisfied sigh, and then heard the rustling of paper behind her. She stopped, turned and discovered David Sharpen, a new phlebotomist working on the seventh floor, standing nearby. He had a blood sample in his left hand and the paperwork in his right. She was surprised that he'd run the sample down himself, and she had no idea how long he'd been standing there.

"How long have you been standing there?" she asked.

"You certainly are focused today."

"I am."

"Can we get this out by the end of the day?"

"What do you need?"

"They want a basic metabolic panel, but especially the glucose."

"That shouldn't be a problem," Rebecca said. She took the test tube and the paperwork. She began preparing the sample, then looked up to find David Sharpen still standing in her tiny corner of the lab, his elbow bumping into the microwave.

"Do you want to get a drink after work?" he asked.

Rebecca set down the sample. She was very surprised, although not so much by David Sharpen's invitation as by her realization that she could, indeed, go with this man, after work, for a drink. The thought that there was nothing stopping her made her conclude that at one point there must have been. Searching her mind, Rebecca quickly understood that this something was Stewart. Not missing him was accompanied by not thinking about him. She no longer needed to keep him in mind as she made each and every decision of her day. Her sudden awareness that she'd unknowingly been doing this for years was unexpected and tinged with sorrow—but discovering that she didn't have to do it anymore was exceedingly joyful.

This sequence of thoughts came to Rebecca quickly, one right after the other, while she stared at the short grey carpet. At the edge of her sightline was David Sharpen's right shoe. It was black leather, a fashionable shape and highly polished. Rebecca raised her gaze upwards until she looked him in the eyes. "Yes," she said. "I'd quite like that."

David Sharpen felt Rebecca's conflicted emotions and then he felt them suddenly resolve. He concluded that she must be on the rebound and this made him smile broadly.

~

Opening her eyes, Rebecca saw that the ceiling was the wrong colour. It was cream; the one she'd woken up under for the preceding twenty-seven months was whiter. She sat up quickly, but it was only after she looked to her right and saw the bleeding heart tattoo on his left shoulder that the events of the evening returned to her. She felt happy. She pulled up the covers, tucked the sheet under her chin and waited for the good feeling to pass.

To her surprise, it remained. Confident that guilt and regret were on their way, and in an effort to hasten their arrival, she turned onto her side. She gently traced her fingers down David Sharpen's back. But her feeling of well-being remained. She let her fingers continue to travel, and her happiness proved to be surprisingly resilient.

The large digital alarm clock on his bedside table told Rebecca she had ninety minutes to get to work, but since she couldn't remember exactly what part of town she was in, it was impossible to estimate how long her commute would be. Climbing from his bed, Rebecca silently collected her clothing. In the bathroom, she turned the hot water tap until it was just a trickle, then washed. She dressed and wrote a warm, friendly note, which she left on the kitchen table. With a great effort to make no sound, Rebecca walked to the apartment door, unlocked it and left.

Even on the other side of David Sharpen's door, Rebecca still felt good about herself. This positive sense of self remained as she got into her car and drove away. It was still there when she got to work. It even remained when she made a special trip up to the seventh floor just to walk past David Sharpen's station, broadly returning his smile.

When she got home from work, Rebecca sat at her kitchen table, feeling better than she'd felt in years. She dialled Stewart's number and was surprised that, even as it began to ring, she still felt no guilt, shame or remorse.

"Hello?" Stewart said.

"Are you working on the boat?"

"I'm manning the front desk. We have guests! Two of them. They're a bit strange. They're supposed to be rainmakers. Are you feeling any better?"

"Actually, I'm feeling really good."

"You sound good."

"I might even be fantastic."

"You sound a bit weird, though."

"Maybe it's just because I'm so good."

"Maybe."

"It's been awhile since I've felt this good."

"True."

"Listen—I've got something I want to ask you," Rebecca said. Her tone was exceedingly casual.

"What?" he asked, warily.

"What do you think of fresh starts?"

"What do you mean?"

"Fresh starts. Are you for them?"

"That question's too big. I mean, everyone's for them in principle."

"Okay. Let me rephrase. Do you think it's cowardly, or courageous, to get rid of your past and start all over again?"

"Why are you asking me this?"

"Don't get defensive."

"Well, obviously I think it's courageous. What do you think I'm doing here?"

Rebecca was silent. She knew he believed he was telling the truth. "Stewart," she said. "This really helped."

"Rebecca? Don't do this again. Tell me what's going on!"

"Hey, Stewart," Rebecca said. "Goodbye."

Closing her phone, she set it on the kitchen table. She walked to her car and drove directly to E.Z. Self Storage.

25

Completion is just the beginning

Behind the front desk of the Prairie Embassy Hotel, Stewart continued to look at the telephone before setting it on the desk and pushing it away. After sitting motionless for some time, he began cleaning off the desk. He put weeks-old newspapers in the trash. He put bookmarks in the four different novels he was in the middle of reading and stacked them neatly, according to size. He gathered all the plates, carried them into the kitchen and pushed the leftover food into the garbage. Washing each dish by hand, he dried them and put them away in the cupboard before returning to the front desk.

Stewart sat down and looked at the telephone, which did not ring, and decided that tonight was the night he'd finish the sailboat. For months, Stewart had been working at a leisurely pace, but in truth there wasn't much left to do.

Heading out to the boat and stepping onto the deck, he turned on the lights, took up his hammer and finished nailing the trim around the cabin, both inside and out.

Next he applied the final coat of fibreglass waterproofing to the hull. Just before the sun rose, Stewart attached the tackle to the mast, fastened the sail and raised it.

Sitting with the rudder in his hand, Stewart looked starboard at the reds and oranges on the horizon, but he couldn't think about anything other than Rebecca. For three years he had waited for one of two things: for her to ask him to come back, or for her to say goodbye and mean it. Now that she'd chosen the latter, he didn't know what came next. He felt a freedom, although one so expansive it was threatening. But more than anything else he felt empty and sad. A dry wind blew over his face, and he looked up just as the wind caught the sail, filling it. But the boat remained motionless on the parched Prairie soil.

26

The physical impossibility of fresh starts

Rebecca pulled open the padlock, took it off the door
and put it in her pocket. She began taking boxes out of
unit #207 and placing them in the hallway. When every
box was out of the storage area, Rebecca arranged them
in chronological order. When she was done, they sat
side by side in a line that snaked down the hallway and
around the corner, where it stopped fewer than three feet
from the elevator.

The boxes closest to the storage unit held the earliest
moments of her life. The boxes farthest away contained
the most recent ones. Only after Rebecca had double-
checked the sequence, moving a few boxes here and a
few boxes there, did she begin loading them into the
elevator.

Using boxes to keep the doors open, Rebecca filled
the elevator completely, leaving no room for herself.
Reaching in, she hit the button for the first floor and
ducked out as the doors were closing. She ran down the
stairs, arriving before the elevator. She could not find the

dolly and was forced to carry each box down the first floor hallway and outside, where she lifted it up and threw it into the Dumpster.

When she'd emptied the elevator, Rebecca rode it to the second floor and loaded it again. She repeated this cycle nine times, until every single box and every single keepsake she'd collected since shortly after she'd turned seven years old was inside the Dumpster.

Rebecca reached into her pocket and took out the padlock. She threw the lock into the Dumpster and closed the lid. Immediately, the pain in her chest began. It was excruciating, far worse than the pain she'd felt for the loss of Stewart's objects, or Lisa's—worse than both those pains combined. She looked at her chest, convinced that something had been ripped out of it, then collapsed to the ground. Every muscle in her body tightened. Her fingers curled into her palms, and her nails cut tiny lines into her flesh. She couldn't breathe. Then the pain stopped. It took her almost five minutes to catch her breath, but then she stood up, walked to her car and started the engine. She looked left and right before exiting the parking lot and pulling onto Broadview Avenue. She checked both her rear-view and side mirrors before changing lanes. She drove responsibly, her hands gripping the wheel at the ten and two positions.

She rolled down the window and played the radio loudly, but it wasn't enough—she was still falling asleep. Paying to park her car, Rebecca hailed a cab. She had barely given the driver her address before she fell asleep in the back seat.

When the driver woke her up, telling her they'd arrived, Rebecca paid, unlocked her front door and went directly to the couch. She fell asleep quickly, unaware that she'd left her front door wide open.

PART EIGHT

The Fear of God

Lewis III

27

Louder than sound

Lewis attempted to focus on the feeling of the carpet against his bare feet and not on the fact that every time he closed his eyes he saw the giant frog. He got out of bed and walked to the window. He looked down at the street. He moved back to the bed, lay down, turned onto his stomach, then his side, and then watched the clock on the bedside table turn to 6:01 a.m.

He couldn't stop thinking about the frogwoman. It wasn't just that he'd talked to her, or that he'd seen her twice, in two different cities. These facts were minor compared to the key chain he'd held since she handed it to him. Lewis looked at the family portrait. Lisa stood to the left of her mother, who was seated. Rebecca was on the other side of the chair, and their significantly taller father stood behind it, benevolently hovering over them all. Lewis continued to stare at the key chain and reached a conclusion he felt was undeniable: its presence was a message, simply and undeniably stated, that the unbelievable must be believed.

Lewis kept the key chain firmly gripped in his right hand as he dressed, left his suite and began looking for the woman who claimed to be God. Realizing that each time she'd appeared he'd been waiting, Lewis began to wait. He waited all morning in the emergency room of Grace General Hospital. At 1:30 he moved to Gus's Barbershop, then to a chair outside the manager's office at the Toronto Dominion Bank on Portage. He waited in a bus shelter in front of the CBC Building, in a dentist's office on the sixth floor of a building he couldn't name and on a bench outside the Winnipeg Art Gallery. Just after 4:00 p.m., Lewis was in the waiting room of the law offices of Aikins, MacAulay & Thorvaldson, on the thirtieth floor of the Commodity Exchange Tower, when he saw her for the fourth time.

The woman who claimed to be God passed so close to where Lewis was sitting that he could have touched her. Her hair was in pigtails that stuck out from the sides of her head. She wore bicycle shorts that revealed too much. Her shoes had metal clasps on the bottom that made her steps click as she walked across the floor. Tucked under her arm was a large manila envelope. Lewis watched as Lisa handed it to the receptionist, waited for the receipt to be signed and walked back through the waiting room, passing as close to Lewis as she had the first time.

Lewis watched her stand in the foyer, waiting for an elevator. She pressed the down button and crossed her arms. Her posture was horrible. When the doors opened, Lewis stood up and ran as hard as he could. Turning his body sideways, he slipped between the doors just as they were closing. There were eight people in the tiny elevator, and everyone was standing very close. Lewis stood beside Lisa, but a floor passed before she recognized him.

"Hey! It's you."

"You're a bike courier?"

"Very observant, Lewis."

Their conversation stopped when the elevator did. The doors opened. Two more men got in. Lisa and Lewis moved to the back. He felt her breath on his face. He reached out his index finger. He softly stroked her cheek and then took hold of her wrist with his right hand. He squeezed. His grip tightened. All colour drained from his face, and it was suddenly significantly easier for him to accept that this woman was God than it was to believe that a giant green frog had asked him for directions. Or that the ghost of his wife had given him advice in his hotel room. Although crude and vulgar, she was undeniably real, and stepping into her delusion, if it was one, seemed profoundly easier than remaining inside his.

"Is this the best you can do?" he asked.

"Lewis, you're hurting me."

"Is this really the best you can do?"

"What are you talking about?"

The shoulders of everyone in the elevator had stiffened. When the doors opened, they exited like a school of fish. Although there were people waiting outside, not one of them entered. The doors closed, and Lewis and Lisa were alone in the elevator.

"Are you talking about being a bike courier? 'Cause it's a pretty good job."

"I'm talking about everything."

Lisa's eyes became very wide, then very narrow. She shook Lewis's grip from her wrist, extended her index finger and executed a single, precise jab to the doors-open button. The doors opened. Taking firm hold of his hand, she led him out of the elevator and pulled him through the lobby and out the large glass doors. Lewis began to lose feeling in his hand. He rushed to keep up with her. Just outside the building, at the top of a flight of concrete steps, she stopped. "Let me tell you a little something about Christianity," she said.

"I'm not Christian."

"The only thing your book got right, and here it is, pay attention," Lisa said, unexpectedly cuffing Lewis on the back of the head. "Is that man was created in my image. Understand?"

"No. No, I don't," Lewis said, although it came out as "Wo. Wo, I thon't," as he'd bitten the tip of his tongue when she hit him on the back of the head.

"Look at me," Lisa said. "I am frail and weak and fragile. And therefore so are you. Therefore so is the world."

Lewis didn't say a word. He stood on the front steps of the Commodity Exchange Tower, watching the street. On the sidewalk immediately in front of him were an inconsolable toddler and a mother running out of patience. Lewis felt for the toddler. He felt for the mother. He wanted to cover his ears before either of their screams got louder, but then he discovered he didn't need to. A city bus stopped at the corner and Lewis heard the brakes squeal but not the doors opening or the people getting of. The conversation of two office workers walking past him disappeared. He looked at Lisa and saw her mouth moving, but she made no sound. He heard no sounds at all.

28

Obscurity is a privilege

Lewis had been deaf for twenty-nine hours, the last three of which he'd spent sitting at the bar in the Palm Room, unable to hear the piano player and finding this wonderful. Not being able to hear meant he didn't have to listen. He was no longer forced to notice the symmetrical sharpness of squealing bus brakes, or the concise melody of an elevator door opening, or the ramshackle perfection of a slightly out-of-tune piano played by a slightly inebriated man wasting his talent. Without sound, the world was a muted television that Lewis could watch or ignore as he pleased. He felt perfect in his perfectly silent world until, having set his glass on the bar, he noticed a tiny version of his wife swimming in his drink.

Lewis watched as she broke the surface and climbed the ice cubes to the top of the glass. She jumped, landed on the bar and ran towards a martini glass filled with toothpicks. Her steps left behind footprints that looked like single drops of water. Approaching the martini glass, she slammed her body against the stem, tipping it over and spilling the toothpicks. As Lewis watched, she began pushing the toothpicks across the bar. He didn't immediately realize that she was spelling.—

"Have to what? Be clear. Be more specific. I have to what?" Lewis said.

The toothpicks were slightly longer then she was. He found it very hard to watch her struggle, but he didn't want to get in her way. Lewis feared she would disappear before conveying her message. Hovering over the bar, Lewis watched the tiny version of his wife continue to spell. She pushed toothpicks this way and that. Finally, she stopped, stepped back and looked up at him, clearly exhausted. She had spelt:

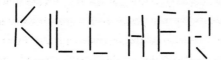

"Ah, baby. What are you saying? What are you saying?"

Lewis felt a tug on his sleeve and recognized the bitten fingernails and purple polish. He looked back down at the bar, but the tiny version of his wife was gone. Jerking his arm to remove the hand, he scattered the toothpicks. He took long strides out of the Palm Room, resisting the urge to run.

He headed towards the elevator. Glancing over his shoulder, he saw that the woman who claimed to be God was following him, and he quickened his pace. He reached the elevators and pushed the up button. All four of the doors remained closed. Lewis pressed the button again, and then pressed it repeatedly. The elevators remained closed. Lisa continued her approach. With as much composure as possible, Lewis turned from the elevators and jogged to the revolving doors and out of the hotel.

≈

The night his wife died, Lewis had fallen asleep in front of the television. Something—he wasn't sure what—had woken him. It was still dark, although he couldn't judge whether it was late at night or early in the morning. He turned off the television, and the resulting silence caused a slight panic. The house was completely still, as if everything had been unplugged, and Lewis sat in this stillness, not liking it. These feelings intensified until Lewis closed his eyes and put his fingers in his ears. He did not know how long he stayed like that, but he jumped when he felt his wife's hand on his shoulder, although he didn't take his fingers out of his ears.

The apartment they'd returned to after the tour was smaller than many of the hotel rooms they'd stayed in. As The Impostors, they'd played medium-sized venues in fourteen countries, as well as opening for The Voltage on eight stadium dates along the eastern coast of the United States. Both Lewis and Lisa described the tour as a success, but there was one major difference: Lewis called it their first tour, and Lisa their only. She wanted to start working on something new, whereas Lewis believed, strongly, that The Impostors was a once-in-a-lifetime opportunity that they'd be stupid not to exploit. They'd been home for sixteen days, and the tension between them had slowly but persistently increased.

"Come to bed," Lisa said. Lewis took his fingers out of his ears. "Come to bed," she repeated.

"Sure?"

"Yes."

Lewis walked up the stairs behind her, keeping a loose grip on her hand. She got into bed. Lewis got into bed beside her, but he did not take off his clothes. The alarm clock on the nightstand ticked. This ticking was consistent, and it made Lewis feel safe. "I'm just kinda lost," he said.

"I know."

"We made so much money. We should do it again."

"But we didn't do it for the money."

"I know."

"It's not really about the money, is it?"

"No."

"What is it, then?" Lisa asked. When he didn't answer, she waited. She thought he'd fallen asleep, but then he spoke.

"Even though I know this is fake, I still like it better than what I really am. I'm afraid of being normal again."

"You're afraid of being in the audience."

"That's a good way to put it."

"What makes you afraid of that?"

"I don't know."

"You should find out," she said. "And you should take off your clothes."

Lewis did as Lisa suggested. He turned so his toes touched her ankles and fell asleep thinking everything was, or would be, fine.

At the top of the hotel steps, Lewis began to run. He pushed through a wedding party exiting a limo and went west on Broadway. Looking over his shoulder, he saw Lisa knock a bridesmaid to the ground, then continue her pursuit. By Smith Street, the pain in his side was immense, but he continued running. By Donald Street, the tightness at the top of his legs was overwhelming, but he ignored it. At Hargrave Street, Lewis looked over his shoulder. Lisa looked angry. By Edmonton Street, she was furious, and she'd begun closing the gap between them.

Having reached the Manitoba Legislative Building, Lewis was cutting across the lawn when Lisa tackled him from behind. His upper body struck the grass with considerable force, ripping the stitching in the shoulder of his jacket. His face slid through the grass, which smelled like it had recently been cut. With surprising strength, Lisa flipped Lewis onto his back. She pinned his shoulders with her knees. Lewis struggled but could not move.

Lisa leaned down until her face was very close to his. "Your wife dies and I'm supposed to care? I've never even met her!" she yelled, her spit landing on Lewis's nose and eyelids. "I didn't kill your wife. I'm not making it so things don't work out for you. I'm sick of being blamed for everything!"

Lewis watched her mouth open and close, and then shut his eyes to avoid the spray. Feeling her knees digging deeper into his shoulders, he opened his eyes. Her face was so close to his that Lewis couldn't focus on it.

"But at least I'm not running around putting a beginning, middle and end on everything," she said, letting go of his collar. She exhaled and then leaned towards him again, so close that their noses touched. "Have you people never noticed that there's a central flaw? No? Here comes the clue—the only difference between a happy ending and a sad ending is where you decide the story ends."

Out of breath, Lisa rolled off Lewis. She pulled down her dress and lay on her back, panting.

Lewis, of course, had heard none of it, and he continued to wonder what she'd said. "Lisa?" he asked.

But Lisa did not turn to look at him. Instead, she stood up and began walking away, without looking over her shoulder. Lewis noticed a strange thing: although Lisa continued to get smaller, the objects around her did not. It did not look like she was receding into the distance, but like she was walking in place while decreasing in size.

"Lisa!" Lewis screamed.

Lisa still did not reply. She got smaller and smaller, and when she disappeared, so did Lewis's sight. First primary colours, then secondary colours, then all shades of grey an then all shades of white, until only black remained.

He sat on the lawn of the Manitoba Legislative Building, blinking and rubbing his eyes, but he remained completely blind.

PART NINE

With the Grace Water Wished it Had

Aby III

29

Thrum

Aberystwyth spent the day she arrived at the Prairie Embassy Hotel within a twenty-foot radius of the white Honda Civic, during which time her mother failed to make a second appearance. To pass the time, Aby listened to music on the car radio, tried to acclimatize her legs and read parts of the Aquatic Bible she'd never read before. She discovered that Síðriin music was discordant, her legs were unwilling to accept the demands of gravity and, as far as the Aquatic Bible was concerned, she definitely hadn't left the best parts to the last. For hours she watched a Síðri make tiny changes to a shack he was building beside the river. Even though Aby was in the middle of what she believed to be the most dramatic event of her life, she was completely bored.

That night, after taking great pains to clean the apple from the windshield and hood, Aby slept on top of the white Honda Civic since it was too hot to sleep inside it. Stretching across the hood and resting her back against the glass was much cooler and significantly more comfortable. Aby wondered why she hadn't thought of it before. Four of her five nights on the road she'd slept folded into the back seat or cramped behind the wheel with her legs pressed against the dashboard.

But something much more significant than comfort resulted from this position: the slight upward tilt of Aby's head created the perfect angle for watching the stars. Pabbi had described them in great detail, but she had forgotten all about it, and now they dazzled her completely. The clear, cloudless Prairie night sky was as beautiful as anything she'd seen underwater. Aby started to count the stars, but quickly gave up. As her legs dangled over the front edge of the hood and she continued to stare upwards, Aberystwyth managed to achieve something she never had before: *thrum*.

Aquatics believe that thrum is a meditative state that can diminish the distance to enlightenment, a sort of metaphysical shortcut. This highly coveted, yet nearly impossible, state allows you to see the events of your life as if they were someone else's. As Aby remained on the hood of the stolen white Honda Civic, looking up, she became able to see her concerns and troubles, her successes and failures, her weaknesses and strengths, as if they belonged to a stranger. Aby, however briefly, was able to see her life not as its star but as its audience.

She recalled the end of each of her significant relationships and then separated what was her fault and what was theirs. She worked through career decisions, friendships that had ended badly and opportunities missed. She saw her mistakes and did not flinch. She recognized her victories and did not gloat. She made observations about her character. Things that would normally have made her feel pathetic and weak became simply things to improve. Her skin turned a deep, rich green that in the moonless Prairie evening appeared almost black.

And then she began to think of her mother. Things for Aby were never the same after her mother's excommunication. Being stuck in a hick town like Nowwlk had been at least novel while her mother's fame increased, but to be stuck there as an outcast was completely intolerable. Yet when they moved back to Alisvín-bær, things didn't get any better. Even in a city as large as this one, her mother's infamy preceded them. Neither of her parents could find work. Aby watched as they started to fight more and more often, trying to hide it from her less and less. Then her mother started coming home later and later in the evening. Although they tried to hide it, Aby knew her parents had begun sleeping in separate beds. Soon they were rarely in the same room, and when they were, both her mother and her father were stiff and formal.

One night Aby woke up to the sounds of them fighting. Their voices were louder and carried more anger than usual. Creeping out of bed, Aby swam to the top of the stairs and listened. When her parents begin to talk in whispers, she snuck to the first landing. She couldn't make out every word, but the one she did hear was "unwatered". Aby returned to her bed, but she did not sleep.

Three days later, Aby came home and found two

suitcases just inside the front door. One was her mother's. The other was hers. Stepping into the foyer, Aby closed the door with force, which brought her mother swimming down from the second floor. Margaret did not speak as she descended. She watched the webbing between her fingers. On the main floor, she bobbed very close to Aby, but they both looked at their feet. Finally, Margaret looked up, although her daughter did not. "Aby, I have to go," Margaret said.

"You can't let them do this to you."

"It's not about them. It's what I have to do."

"What about us?"

"I want you to come with me."

"No way."

"Why won't you?"

"I can't believe you're doing this to me!"

"It's not about you."

"It should be."

"Do you think this is easy for me?"

"Yes," Aby said, and although her arms remained crossed, her jaw unclenched and the edges of her gills quivered.

"I have to go."

"No, you don't!" Aby yelled. Grabbing her mother's suitcase, she swam into the living room and raised it over her head. The contents spilled out. Her mother's clothes floated through the water.

"I have to go," Margaret said.

"It's not right. You'll die there. You'll be *sála-glorsol-tinn*!"

"It's not true."

"What if it is?"

Margaret did not reply. One of her dresses floated in front of her, but Margaret did not reach out for it. She turned, opened the front door and swam through it. Aby watched as the door closed, then looked down at her suitcase sitting in the hallway by itself.

Aberystwyth's *thrum* concluded with this memory. She came out of it blinking. Less than a minute had passed. She did not move, not even her head. Although her *thrum* had shown her many things, one question remained unanswered: Was she here to help her mother, or herself?

30

The great storm

Anderson and Kenneth Richardson spent three days and two nights on the roof of the Prairie Embassy Hotel, waiting for the perfect cloud. They each spotted several clouds that might do the job, but let them pass. Holding binoculars to their eyes, the rainmakers continued watching different corners of the sky, Kenneth surveying the west and Anderson the east. Then a cloud came in from the north that was so large both men saw it in the edges of their binoculars and lowered their glasses to see it with their own eyes.

It was, of course, a cumulonimbus, and was breathtaking in its grandeur. Its slate-flat bottom hung low, no higher than fifteen hundred feet. From there, it towered upwards, easily breaking sixty thousand feet. Fold after fold of white towered higher and higher, billowing like a plush atomic cloud; that it remained airborne seemed improbable. It crept towards them as if under its own power. Their heads followed its path until its shadow was on top of them and the sun became invisible.

The rainmakers were inspired to an awe that bordered on the religious—it was a rare wonder, one that many wouldn't even have noticed, let alone revered. Then they got to work. Kenneth put his fingers into his mouth and whistled. Starlings seemed to materialize out of thin air, gathering around him. Moving with quick, practiced motions he began attaching pouches to birds. Anderson, who had already circled his car batteries, began connecting the wires. Sixteen lengths of copper led from the positive and negative poles of each battery to the kite. When the middle of the cloud was precisely overhead, Kenneth released the starlings, the birds straining under the weight of the added silver iodide. Anderson released his kite, the wind carrying it back and forth.

The birds and the kite disappeared into the cloud at exactly the same moment. For a full second there was silence, then a blinding light flashed through the cloud, accompanied by a sound so loud that both rainmakers covered their ears. Looking up, their hands still held tightly to the sides of their heads, they saw the remains of the kite carried away by a sudden and growing wind. Then starlings began to fall. Dead birds, one after another, landed between father and son. They were followed shortly by the first drops of rain.

31

A lesser form of matricide

Aby's attention was so taken by the flash of light and the deafening clap of thunder that had come from the sky directly above the Prairie Embassy Hotel that she jumped when she heard the knock on the driver's side window. First she noticed the rain that fell, then her eyes focused on her mother. Margaret rolled her eyes. Aby rolled down the window.

"This will help," Margaret said. She raised her right hand, which held a cane.

"To what?"

"To walk. You use it like a third leg. For balance."

To demonstrate, Margaret circumnavigated the stolen white Honda Civic, showing how the cane could be used to support her weight between steps. She stopped when she was behind the driver's door again. Aby opened the door and tentatively twisted her thin legs to the ground, which the rain was already moistening. Refusing the cane, she took a full, confident step. She took a second step, followed by a third. Then she fell, her body raising a small cloud of dust as she landed.

Margaret tossed the cane. It landed inches from Aby's head, raising another cloud of dust, albeit much smaller. Margaret watched her daughter, lying face down in the dirt, struggling to right herself. She was, Margaret thought, a quintessential example of the dangers of dogma. Here was a creature who God had created with the ability to breathe both water and air, to swim and to run, but she'd spent her whole life experiencing only half of her gifts. It reminded Margaret of the Christians she knew who were scared of their genitals, or the scientists who could accept only a rational explanation as the right one.

Without looking up, Aby grabbed the cane and used it to stand. She then followed her mother towards the Prairie Embassy Hotel.

"This is the first rain we've had in fifty-nine days," Margaret said, her voice conveying regret that the drought was over. Everything Margaret loved about the Prairie Embassy Hotel, she'd loved even more during the drought. She loved the dry heat. She loved the cracks it caused in the mud of the riverbed. She loved breathing the heat into her lungs and feeling the dirt turn to dust beneath her footsteps. It was all so infused with the qualities of land. But now it was all just becoming mud again.

As they climbed the steps to the lobby, Margaret studied Aby's reflection in the glass of the front door. She could not deny that seeing her daughter healthy and alive felt extraordinarily good, a relief she had not expected to feel. Inside the hotel, this feeling grew, but Margaret remained wary. She reminded herself that her daughter most likely remained devoutly Aquatic, which meant Aby was here with only one thing on her mind.

As Aby followed her mother into the lobby, she was struck by how large it was, and she stopped to take everything in. The hotel had not looked this big from outside. The decorations were elegant, if in decline. Polished mahogany banisters lined the twin staircases, which climbed the north and south walls; there was no elevator. A vacuum cleaner lay motionless and unplugged in the middle of the floor. The room smelled strongly of fish. At the back of the lobby, past the front desk, was a small open door, which Margaret had already walked through. Aby followed, finding herself in a glass porch.

Light flooded the room. The porch overlooked the Red River, a body of water Aby hadn't discovered, despite sitting so close to it. Only now did she realize that the structure the Siðri was building wasn't a shack or a tiny house, as she'd assumed, but a boat. The river didn't look big enough to float it, though, a situation that was more pronounced now that the Red was a trickle of its former self. The distance between the water and the banks was considerable. These banks were hard, with deep eggshell cracks running through them, but the rain had already begun to soften them. As she looked at the river, Aby's gills flicked open and shut repeatedly.

"Do you want tea?" Margaret asked.

"I brought you some *stryim*."

"Let's have that!" Margaret said.

This was the moment Aby had prepared for, had

thought through over and over again since she was a *tysnner*, which for humans would be a teenager. It was, in fact, a moment Aby had waited seventeen years for. Reaching into her front pocket, she began to withdraw a carefully wrapped package of her mother's favourite beverage. But it was stuck. Aby pulled harder, which succeeded in freeing the package, but purple leaves flew onto the wooden floor of the lobby. So did her Bible. The book landed spine down and opened itself, displaying pages 204 and 205.

"I knew it!" Margaret said.

"Just listen."

"Get out!"

"You must have had some. The rust? Have you?"

"Get out!"

"Mom, I still love you!"

"Not enough!" Margaret yelled. She picked up what was closest at hand, which was the telephone, and threw it. The phone travelled through the air only as far as the cord would allow, then snapped backwards, crashing at her feet. When Margaret turned to find a second projectile, Aby dropped to her hands and knees and began crawling out of the lobby.

Aby crawled down the stairs and through the rain and the gravel to the white Honda Civic. She sat inside the car and listened to the rain strike the metal hood and the roof. When she was sure enough time had passed, Aby walked back inside the Prairie Embassy Hotel, taking awkward steps. There were no sounds of occupancy. Her mother was not in the lobby. She was not on the back porch. Aby found her slumped over the kitchen table, a teacup still in her hand and a purple stain on her blouse.

Aby had, of course, drugged the *stryim*, knowing that her mother could not resist it. She had been particularly worried about the time between when Margaret consumed the drug and when it took effect. It could have hit her while was she was standing. She could have fallen, breaking a hip or worse. That this had not happened caused Aby to push a sigh of relief through her gills. She removed the teacup from Margaret's hands and, bending low, lifted her mother over her shoulder.

Aby's upper body remained strong, and she had no problems picking her mother up, but she remained unsteady as she walked. Taking small, slow steps and periodically setting Margaret down, Aby carried her mother to the white Honda Civic. The rain had softened the ground, which made each step that much more precarious. The journey of no more than fifty metres took ten minutes.

Aby placed Margaret in the passenger seat. She fastened the seat belt. She tugged it to make sure it was secure and adjusted the tilt of her mother's head so she wouldn't wake up with a kink in her neck. Then she pushed the wet hair off Margaret's face. "I'm sorry," Aby said.

Returning to the driver's seat, Aby started the car. Performing a three-point turn, she aimed the white Honda Civic towards the main road. Filled with doubt about whether she was doing the right thing, Aby looked for the hotel in the rear-view mirror, but the rain was now falling so hard that she couldn't see a thing.

PART TEN

The Book of Doubt and Endings

32

The purpose of speech

Lying on her back in the grass, Rebecca was looking up at the branches of a maple tree when a shadow crossed her face. To her left was a girl, four or five years old, who was wearing jeans and a yellow T-shirt. On her T-shirt was an iron-on decal from a television program that had been popular during Rebecca's childhood. Sitting on her knees, Rebecca was exactly the same height as the girl. In the little girl's palm were two cookies. One was clearly chocolate chip. The other looked like it had flakes of coconut in it.

Rebecca was not confused about whether she was dreaming or remembering, since she was certain she was doing both.

"Which one do you want?" the girl asked Rebecca, impatiently, as if she'd already asked this question several times.

"What?" Rebecca asked.

"That's not what you say."

"Are you talking about the cookies?"

"You shouldn't be talking at all."

"No?"

"No."

"I'm sorry," Rebecca said. "I don't follow."

"You've completely forgotten this, haven't you?"

"I'm a little confused."

"You shouldn't be talking," the girl said. She stomped her right foot.

Rebecca looked at the girl and didn't say anything.

"That's better," the girl said. She raised her arms higher. Rebecca looked at the cookies.

"Which one?" the girl demanded.

Rebecca still didn't know what to say, so she said nothing. She looked down and realized she was no longer on her knees. But although she was now standing, she was still the same height as the girl.

"It's snack time," the girl said.

Rebecca looked around and realized it was her first day of kindergarten. Nap time had just ended, and Rebecca and the girl had been the last ones to roll up their mats. As a result, they had been the last ones to get to the snack table, where only two cookies were left, one chocolate chip, the other coconut.

The girl looked expectantly at Rebecca.

"You stole the last two cookies?" Rebecca asked.

"But Mrs. Wilson caught me," she said. "She saw what I did, and now she's making me share with you. You get to choose which one you want."

"I'm still blanking."

"Rebecca, this is a very important memory for you."

"I believe you."

"I can't believe you don't remember."

"I don't."

"Nothing?"

"Not much."

"Do you remember that you haven't learned to talk yet?"

"I know I didn't speak until I was five."

"Exactly. And this is it. This is where you speak your very first word. Come on Rebecca—people thought you might be retarded."

"I'm sorry."

"Smell them."

"What?"

"Smell them," the girl said. She shook her palms. The cookies bounced.

Rebecca leaned down to smell the chocolate chip one. Then she smelled the coconut. She breathed in both smells deeply. "Your name is Heather."

"That's it."

Rebecca smelled the cookies again. "And you want the chocolate chip," she said.

"Who wouldn't?"

"But you're lying to me."

"Am I?"

"Yes. It was me who stole the cookies," Rebecca said. "And I've been caught and I'm very frightened. It's me who's being punished; you get to choose first."

"Maybe."

"And I've never learned to speak because I've never

had to. Everyone feels my feelings, so they already know what I want."

"But not me."

"No—I'm still broadcasting, you're just not listening."

"Well, I am five," Heather said.

"I've never met anyone like you. You're too preoccupied with your own feelings to have anything to do with mine."

"Then why would I ask you which one you want?"

"Because you don't know what you want. You're not sure which cookie is better. You'll want whichever one I want. And I've just figured that out."

"So which one do you want?"

"Coconut."

"So do I," Heather said. She held up the chocolate chip cookie. Rebecca reached out, took it and began to eat it. Heather started eating the coconut cookie. Both were happy with their decision.

"See, that's the thing, Rebecca," Heather said, her mouth full of cookie. "The only reason you learned to talk was to lie. And this is where it all started, where you started trying to hide what you really feel. I can't believe you've forgotten it. You gotta wonder about that."

"Yes. It does feel important."

Heather nodded. She turned and walked away, and in a dozen steps she was gone.

Rebecca looked down. She was standing in two inches of water, and the water was rising. Soon it was past her hips, up to her neck. Rebecca breathed in, her lungs filling with water. She shut her eyes as the water covered the top of her head.

Rebecca woke up coughing. She listened to the world around her, which felt much too still. Sitting on the edge of the bed, she looked at her clock. It was 9:00 a.m., but Rebecca did not realize it was Sunday, not Saturday, and that she'd been sleeping for thirty-four hours.

33

Marble countertops and the beginnings of despair

Just after 3:00 a.m., two members of the Winnipeg Police Service spotted Lewis sitting on the lawn of the Legislative Building. They assumed he was a vagrant who needed to be moved along, but changed their minds when they saw how well groomed he was. But when Lewis failed to respond to verbal prompts, they each took hold of one of Lewis's arms and forced him to stand.

"My name is Lewis Taylor. I cannot see or hear. I'm staying at the Fort Garry Hotel. Please help me."

The hold on his arms did not loosen, and Lewis was led to the back seat of a car. He was unable to tell how much time passed before the car stopped. He continued to wait without speaking and then felt a hand on his elbow. The hand didn't let go of him until he was out of the car and had been led up steps and into a building. He could smell lilies. Remembering the large bouquet that routinely sat on the front desk, Lewis assumed he was inside the Fort Garry. The hand let go, and soon he smelled perfume, and another arm, a woman's, linked through his.

"Is this Beth?" he asked, unaware that his voice was very loud. His question was answered by a gentle squeeze, which he considered a yes. She led him forward and stopped. Running his hand along the wall, he realized he was at the bank of elevators. "Floor sixteen, please!" he shouted, just in case Beth had forgotten.

When he felt the elevator stop, Lewis shook off the hand that held his elbow and walked forward. Knowing that his door was the first on the right, he raised his hand and took tiny steps until he felt the door frame. He pulled his pass card from his wallet. After trying it a number of different ways, he managed to unlock the door.

It took Lewis some time to find the bedroom because he had walked into the bathroom by mistake and didn't realize it until his fingers felt something cold and smooth, which was the mirror. Following the cold granite of the countertop, he left the bathroom and stepped forward until his knees hit the king-sized bed. He took off his shoes and socks, got under the sheets and pulled his legs up to his chest. He experimented with opening his eyes and keeping them closed. But it made no difference. The darkness was just as dark, and this is what terrified him the most.

34

The empty deal

When Margaret awoke, she did not recognize the landscape, the car she was travelling in or, for a moment, her daughter. She remained silent but unfastened her seat belt and turned sideways in the passenger seat. The sound of the windshield wipers filled the car. After looking at her watch and establishing that a little less than thirteen hours had passed since she'd been sitting at her kitchen table drinking *stryim*, Margaret stared at her daughter.

Aberystwyth kept her eyes focused on the wet road. She had been strong enough to steal the white Honda Civic, drive it across the country and drug and kidnap her mother. But one thing she couldn't bring herself to do was tie Margaret up. Whether this was from weakness or compassion, Aby still didn't know.

Aby struggled to keep from showing her panic. She'd thought the drug would keep Margaret asleep for much longer, another fourteen or fifteen hours at least. This would have allowed Aby to get past Toronto, which she'd hoped would be far enough to convince Margaret to continue on to the ocean. As it was, Aby had barely passed the Ontario–Manitoba border. Not knowing what to do next, Aby stared straight ahead. Her gills flicked open and closed. She knew that her mother might attack her at any moment.

Margaret continued staring. They travelled another twenty-seven kilometres in silence. Then Margaret folded her hands in her lap and smiled. Her smile was broad. "Did you think about gas?" she asked.

"What?"

"Did you think it through?"

"Don't underestimate me, Mother."

"But did you think about the gas? Your car—"

"It's not my car."

"Cars need gasoline to operate."

"You think I don't know that?"

"Well, how much do you have?"

"The tank is almost full."

"Is? Or was?"

"Was."

"How long ago was that?"

"About three hours."

"And how long can you go on a full tank?"

"I've done the math."

"How long?"

"Six and a half hours."

Margaret turned in her seat, away from her daughter, her eyes focusing on the drops of rain hitting her window rather than on the scenery. "When your car—"

"It's not my car."

"When this car runs out of gas," Margaret continued, turning again to stare at her daughter, "I will get out and make my way back to my hotel. If you try to stop me, I will punch and kick and bite and scratch. If you continue to try, I will explain to those around me that this strange, green-skinned woman has kidnapped me."

"You're green too."

"Not like you. I've been out of the water so long that my green has faded to almost nothing. I bet you still scare people."

Aby looked in the rear-view mirror.

"I'll tell them you drugged me and took me from my home. You will be prosecuted by their law and confined to a very small box, where you will spend the rest of your life unwatered. You will die, on land, with air in your lungs. Do you understand this?"

"Yes."

"Do you know that I will do this?"

"I do."

"Will you turn around now?"

"No."

"I didn't think so," Margaret said.

The rain continued to fall. The windshield wipers seemed loud. Aby's grip on the steering wheel was very tight. She had discovered one thing she did not like to do in water, and that was drive in it. The rain seemed to be falling more heavily with every kilometre. Aby had to pay close attention to the road, although she continued to steal glances at her mother.

Margaret leaned forward and extended her index

finger to the windshield. Starting in the upper right corner, Margaret traced the crack. When she reached its origin in the centre, she turned towards her daughter, but kept her left fingertip pressed against the glass.

"This is the part of you I've always liked best. I like you bold. I like your stubbornness. You certainly didn't get it from Pabbi," Margaret said. Looking down, she noticed for the first time that there were several bottles of water at her feet. Aby had put them there for her, knowing her mother would be thirsty when she woke up. Opening one of the bottles with her teeth, Margaret pulled three-quarters of its contents into her lungs. Tilting her head back, she pushed the water out of her mouth and through her gills. Making a fountain of herself, Margaret let the water land on her face and eyes and spill down the back of her neck.

"This is what we'll do," Margaret said. "You may keep travelling east. From now until your car runs out of gas, I will listen and you will try to persuade me. You can use any argument you want. I will keep an open mind. Should you succeed, I will willingly return to the water."

Aby turned and studied her mother's face. Her mother was not lying. The deal Margaret was offering was much more than Aby could have hoped for. She knew that her mother, working within the limits of her personality, was being more than reasonable. Aby looked at the fuel gauge; the needle was just below the halfway point.

35

Zimmer's favourite pastime

Zimmer studied all seventeen video monitors until he was sure he was alone in E.Z. Self Storage. He looked at his watch—7:05 a.m. It was rare for anyone to come in this early. Reaching into his right pocket, he pulled out his large set of keys. He flipped through them until he found the one he was looking for: a silver key, slightly smaller and thinner than the rest.

Holding it between the thumb and index finger of his right hand, Zimmer left his office and walked to the first floor of the storage units. Extending the index finger of his left hand, Zimmer tapped each lock as he passed it, leaving a hallway of swinging locks behind him. At the end of the hall he got into the elevator and took it to the third floor. He walked directly to unit #387 and used the silver key to open the padlock.

Once inside, Zimmer began to open boxes. He opened one that was full of winter clothes and wrapped six scarves around his neck. In another box was a cowboy hat, which Zimmer put on his head. He opened boxes filled with antiquated kitchen appliances, textbooks with uncracked spines and children's toys. Then he found ski boots and a pair of cross-country skis in a tall bag and put them on. He clumped down the hallway and back.

Zimmer took off the skis and boots and stepped back into the storage unit. He removed the scarves, the cowboy hat. He put everything back exactly as he'd found it. Leaving the unit, Zimmer looked over his shoulder to make sure he'd gotten everything just right. Satisfied, he turned off the light and locked the door.

Taking the stairs down to the second floor, he found that he was unable to resist stopping at unit #207. He already had the slightly smaller, thinner key between his thumb and forefinger when he saw that the lock was missing. Quickly, Zimmer pulled open the door of unit #207 and discovered that it was empty.

36

The symptoms

Having not yet eaten breakfast, Rebecca peeled three bananas and sliced them on the table. When she opened the refrigerator to get milk, she saw a carton of eggs. Taking out two, she set them on the table and opened the cupboard to get a bowl. Inside the cupboard she saw granola. After pouring the granola into the bowl meant for the eggs, Rebecca returned to the refrigerator and saw a tub of yogurt. With the yogurt in her hand, she turned back to the table and froze, unable to decide if she should add it to the sliced bananas or the granola.

The plastic yogurt container in her hand began to sweat. Rebecca remained where she was, the refrigerator humming behind her. She saw that fruit flies had already found the peels. She knew all she had to do was decide: bananas, granola or eggs. Still she stood there, frozen with indecision, until the phone rang. Picking it up, Rebecca pressed it against her ear.

"Rebecca? Is this Rebecca?"

"This is Rebecca." She recognized the voice but couldn't place it.

"It's Edward."

"Edward Zimmer?"

"That's right."

"Hello, Edward."

"How are you, Rebecca?"

"I'm not so sure, Edward."

"I saw that you cleaned out #207."

"I did."

"How does it feel?"

"I was just trying to figure that out," Rebecca said. She thought about the ways she could answer this question. She was almost positive that she felt very different, but she couldn't be sure she accurately remembered what she had felt like before.

"Rebecca? Are you still there?"

"I'm here," Rebecca said. Her grip on the phone was hurting her hand, so she dropped it, watching it fall to the carpet. She picked up the phone, placed it back on the charger and returned to the kitchen table. Seeing that the refrigerator door was open, she closed it. The phone rang again. She waited until the third ring, then picked it up, although she still did not speak.

"Rebecca?"

"Yes?"

"Maybe we should have a talk. You know? Maybe you should swing by and we can talk. Can you do that for me?"

"Who is this?"

"It's Edward."

"Edward Zimmer?"

"Yes."

"I don't think I'm doing very well, Edward."

"Then you should come see me."

"Where?"

"E.Z. Self Storage."

"Yes. I can do that."

"Do you know where it is?"

"142 Broadview Avenue."

"Do you need directions?"

"I've been there a million times."

"That's true . . ."

"Well, maybe not a million."

"Rebecca, maybe you could just do one thing for me?"

"What's that?"

"Will you take a taxi?"

"Why?"

"Picture turning left, against traffic."

"Oh. Yes. It doesn't matter anyway. I left my car somewhere."

"Do you want me to call a cab for you?"

"No. I'll be okay."

"Can I just make one other suggestion?"

"Yes."

"Wear what you wore yesterday."

Rebecca looked at the peeled and sliced bananas, the box of granola, the eggs and the yogurt.

"Yes," she said. "I think those are both good suggestions, Edward."

"You'll be fine, Rebecca. I promise."

"Okay," Rebecca said. She set the receiver gently in the cradle and stood beside the telephone. She was unable to decide if she believed him or not.

Twenty minutes later, dressed in the clothes she'd worn the day before, Rebecca stood at the southeast corner of Dundas and Ossington, trying to hail a cab. She had debated whether she should walk to the corner and hail one, or call one and wait at home. Unable to decide, she had flipped a coin.

A number of cars passed, but none of them were taxis. This made her angry. But then, half a block away, she spotted an orange car with a sign attached to its roof. Rebecca raised her hand. The taxi approached, then passed without slowing. Watching it continue east on Dundas, Rebecca felt crushing rejection. Tears welled up in her eyes. The feeling was as intense as any she'd ever had—as if she'd just been dumped or passed over for a promotion she richly deserved.

When she saw a second cab, she was too nervous to raise her hand. But as she watched it come closer, the feeling of rejection began to disappear. When the taxi was fifty metres away, she raised her hand, but it, too, drove past her. Rebecca became furious. "You fucker!" she yelled at the driver. She stomped her foot on the ground. She put a piece of nicotine gum in her mouth and chewed ferociously.

Her anger evaporated when the third taxi came into sight. She raised her hand. As the cab slowed down and stopped in front of her, Rebecca was overcome with joy. She began bouncing, jumping up and down on her toes while raising her arms over her head. "Thank you, thank you, thank you!" she said, climbing into the back seat. She sat in the middle, leaning into the gap between the seats. "I'm so happy that you stopped! I'm really, really happy that you stopped."

"Oh, yeah," the driver said, turning on the meter. "Where to?"

"E.Z. Self Storage. Broadview and Queen!"

The driver said no more. The taxi pulled away from the curb. Rebecca looked down at her hands, wondering what she'd just been so happy about.

≈

Edward Zimmer greeted her at the door. *He certainly is tall*, she thought.

"Hello, Rebecca," Zimmer said. He could not gauge Rebecca's emotional state, and this caused him great concern.

"Hello," Rebecca replied.

"Do you know me?"

"You're Edward Zimmer."

"How well do you know me?"

"I met you on April 14th, seven years ago, when I first rented unit #207."

"Are we friends?"

"We're on a first-name basis. That must mean something."

"What does it mean?"

"That we've known each other a long time?"

"Is seven years a long time to know someone?"

"It's longer than I've known most people."

Taking his hands out of his pockets, Zimmer gently set them on Rebecca's shoulders. With tender pressure, he steered her into the back office. Zimmer turned off the video monitors. He closed his laptop and turned off the radio. The room became quiet. The cars travelling on the expressway became audible, and the sound of constant traffic made Rebecca feel safe. Zimmer pulled out a chair for Rebecca, and she sat down.

"You have to describe everything you're feeling," Zimmer said.

"I'm not really feeling anything, Edward."

"What about the small things? How are you reacting to small things?"

"You're right about that. I just wanted to kill a cabby and then I practically kissed the next one."

"And the big things?"

"Like what?"

"Like your sister."

"I don't think I feel anything at all."

"Are you confused?"

"Only when you ask me questions."

"Other than that, nothing?"

"I'm not very good with decisions right now."

"When did you empty unit #207?"

"Two nights ago? Maybe three?"

"And what did you keep?"

"Nothing."

Zimmer gasped. "Nothing?" he asked.

"Nothing."

"No photographs? No souvenirs? Not a high school yearbook or a piece of jewellery?"

"I threw everything away."

"But you must have kept something at home?"

"Everything was here."

"You threw it all in the Dumpster? Around back?"

"Yes."

Zimmer swirled in his chair and looked at the calendar on the wall. It was Tuesday. The garbage should have been picked up Monday night, but there was still a chance. "Wait right here," Zimmer said. "Don't do anything."

"Okay."

"I'm serious, don't do anything. Nothing."

"I'm not a child."

Zimmer did not feel like arguing. Forcing himself not to hurry, he walked across the parking lot behind the building. The Dumpster came into view. The top was flush. It looked empty to Zimmer, but he approached it anyway. He pushed up the lid and looked inside. A yellow plastic bag was stuck to the bottom, along with several pages of newspaper. He let the lid fall, making a loud, metallic crash.

Straightening his tie, Zimmer walked back across the parking lot. He found Rebecca sitting in exactly the same

248

position he'd left her in. She looked up and tried to smile, but once again failed.

Zimmer went straight to the telephone and dialled the number of One Man's Treasures from memory. "Yes, this is Edward Zimmer. E.Z. Self Storage. Client number XET-860. Yes, I'll hold," Zimmer said. Tucking the phone under his chin Zimmer pulled a pack of gum from the inside pocket of his jacket. He unwrapped a piece and put it in his mouth. Then he offered a stick to Rebecca. Rebecca stared at the gum but could not decide whether she wanted a piece or not.

37

Reaching empty

The needle was far below the red bar and Aby had failed to come up with a convincing argument. The engine stalled. Letting the car glide onto the shoulder, Aby turned to look at her mother. With her gills quivering slightly, she spoke. "Mom, would you please let me take you home?" she asked.

They listened to the windshield wipers and the sound of rain on the roof. Margaret looked down at her hands; Aby looked at her mother.

"That's it?" Margaret said. She raised her head and stared at her daughter. "That's all you've got?"

"I left the water for you!"

"About time."

"I've travelled thousands of kilometres."

"I didn't ask you to."

"I risked my soul."

"You think you risked your soul because you came out of the water?"

"Doesn't that mean anything to you?"

"The point of Aquaticism is that it's supposed to teach you *how* to think, not *what* to think."

"What does that mean?"

"I can't believe that you, my own daughter, have never figured that out."

"Tell me!"

"It means you've failed, Aberystwyth. You've failed."

Margaret said nothing more. She leaned back in her seat, reached underneath her and found the ends of her seat belt. With small, careful movements, she buckled herself in.

Aby remained silent. She slumped over the steering wheel. She rested her head in the centre of it, accidentally honking the horn.

"You'll need more gas."

"I have a full can in the trunk."

38

A warning unheeded

Anderson and Kenneth stood shoulder to shoulder in the middle of Mayor Matczuk's office, dripping on the carpet. The sound of the heavy rain hitting the room's only window was loud.

Behind the desk, Mayor Matczuk tented his fingers. Realizing that this gesture was perhaps too dramatic, he put his hands in his lap. He leaned forward in his chair and raised his eyebrows. "We just don't have any proof," he said. He had spent the days since hiring the rainmakers rehearsing this speech, and he was eager to recite his next line. "Yes, it's raining, but can you prove that it was your work? And if it was, which one of you did it?"

"This isn't about that," Anderson said.

"Just listen," Kenneth said.

"I'm sorry, but I'm simply unable to help you boys out."

"Will you just shut up for a second?"

"This is bigger than that."

"You need to evacuate the town."

Matczuk openly laughed at Anderson's suggestion and then looked directly at Kenneth. "He's not serious?" the mayor asked.

"I agree with him completely," Kenneth replied. Although neither father nor son noticed, it was the first time they'd acknowledged each other since they'd stopped working together.

"Well, that's just ludicrous. We won't be doing that."

"Then don't say we didn't warn you," Kenneth said.

"Oh, yes. Yes, yes, yes. I hear your warning. I'll be taking it under great consideration."

Kenneth put his hat back on. Anderson buttoned up his raincoat. Leaving a wet spot on the mayor's carpet, they turned and left They stood just beyond the doorway of the town office and looked up at the rain, which contined to fall harder and harder

39

Room service

Lewis knew that a number of hours had passed, but only because he had become very hungry. Seated on the edge of the bed, he leaned forward slightly. He began searching the top of the bedside table. He knocked over the lamp, then managed to set it upright again. He found the phone and put the receiver to his ear. He reached over to the dial pad but couldn't remember where zero was. He tried to picture its location and became reasonably sure it was the middle button of the bottom row. He pressed that button. He counted to five and began to speak.

"Hello? Hello? Hello? Hello? Hello?" he said, loudly repeating the salutation for fifteen seconds. Knowing that the concierge usually answered the phone on the second ring, he was sure this should be enough. "This is Lewis Taylor in the Vice-Regal Suite," he continued. He spoke quickly, leaving no room for interruption, at a greater volume than was necessary. "I would like room service. A clubhouse sandwich. Fries. Please leave the tray outside the door."

Having ordered food at least twice a day since he'd checked into the hotel, Lewis knew if he had successfully placed the call that his sandwich would arrive in almost exactly thirty minutes. He sat in the middle of the bed and waited. After what felt like thirty minutes, he stood up. He stretched out his arms and made his way to the door.

Opening the door, Lewis crouched in the hallway and felt a tray. He took off the lid. The sandwich was cold. The bread had started to harden. His hunger overwhelmed him, and, holding the door open with his body, Lewis began to eat, taking large bites. He ate quickly, almost savagely. When he felt he'd eaten everything, he backed into the suite, leaving the dishes in the hallway.

40

Mr. Zimmer's warning

Edward Zimmer and Rebecca stood in a small valley of garbage. Rebecca counted the seagulls wandering around the piles of trash and reached fifty-seven before a bulldozer scared them off. Leaning back, she watched the seagulls fly overhead. Her hard hat fell off, but she didn't pick it up. Zimmer's hard hat was also too big for him. He had buttoned his dress shirt up over his nose and tucked the cuffs of his pants into his argyle socks. Running from one pile of garbage to the next, Zimmer kicked small pieces out of the way and lifted larger pieces with the end of a broomstick. Sensing that Rebecca had stopped working, Zimmer turned around. He saw her hard hat on the ground.

"Pick it up!" Zimmer said, his voice muffled by his dress shirt. "They said we had to wear them."

Rebecca did what Zimmer asked. The hard hat slumped forward over her eyes, so she turned it until the peak was at the back. She looked into the distance, where three garbage trucks were unloading. She watched garbage pour out. Rebecca had always thought of garbage trucks as big and the amount of garbage they held to be large, but she no longer thought this. Compared with all the garbage already in the dump, they were depositing very little. She looked down at her feet and kicked a plastic doll head. "This is hopeless," she said. "And it smells really bad. Will you drive me home?" This was the first firm decision she'd made all day.

"No," Zimmer said. He lifted a pair of blue jeans by hooking a belt loop with the broom handle. "We can find them. They're somewhere in here. All we have to do is find them." As Zimmer spoke, he waved the broomstick in the air, making the pants dance.

Rebecca stared.

"We have to find your things."

Rebecca walked across the garbage until she stood beside him. She put her left hand on Zimmer's shoulder, squeezing lightly. Zimmer sighed and his shoulders fell. The sun was setting behind the bulldozers as the operators shut down their machines. Zimmer nodded and Rebecca followed him to his car.

Zimmer parked in front of Rebecca's house and rolled down his window. Rebecca traced the edges of the glove compartment with the tip of her index finger. A couple walked along the sidewalk beside the car, and Zimmer waited until they'd passed before he spoke.

"You know, it's not so uncommon, what you have," he said.

"What do you mean?"

"The emotions. That other people feel what you feel."

"I've never met anyone else who has it."

"You have. You just didn't notice. Or you thought you were really in sync with them. That you just really got them. Everybody likes to think they're empathetic. You know, all the things people think when they meet you."

"Maybe."

"Your solution isn't unique, either. That's why I know how much danger you're in right now," he said. He looked up, looked at Rebecca and then pulled a package of filterless Camels out of his pocket, lighting one with a wooden match. The smoke curled around inside the car before being drawn out the open window. "For years, decades, you've taken your strongest, most personal emotions and stored them outside yourself, inside all those things. But when the objects left you, the emotions left you too. You are now without an emotional past."

"Is that so bad?" Rebecca asked. She saw an emotion flash across Zimmer's face, but she couldn't tell if it was anger or fear.

Zimmer looked at his cigarette, watching the end of it. "I urge you to start creating an emotional history as fast as you can. You need to be feeling significant things. Not just everyday emotions—anger at a parking ticket or whatever. But really deep, true feelings."

"So you've seen this before?"

"I have."

"And what happened to them? In the end?"

"Every case is different."

"Edward . . ."

"You need to believe that every case is different."

"Okay," Rebecca said. She looked at Zimmer, who stared at the speedometer of the motionless car.

"You're about to become emotionally invulnerable," he said. "It will feel safe. It will feel like a good thing. But that's the problem. Who's gonna to make themselves vulnerable if they don't have to? Who's gonna willingly make themselves weaker? But if you don't start feeling real emotions soon, you will quite literally become nothing."

"What do you mean, nothing?"

"You just need to start feeling something. Something meaningful."

"What do you think my chances are?"

"You can do it. I know you can."

"Okay," Rebecca said. She opened the door and stepped onto the sidewalk, then bent down and looked through the window. Zimmer briefly attempted to smile, then started the car. As he drove away, Rebecca realized that he had been crying. She watched her feet on the sidewalk and knew that seeing Zimmer's tears could make her feel sad, even afraid. She also knew she could feel grief and sadness for Lisa, or for losing Stewart, or even for herself if she wanted to, but she didn't have to. It was now a choice.

As she unlocked her front door, she decided to choose not to.

41

The story of the tides

Just before 3:00 a.m., Aby pulled the white Honda Civic into the parking lot of the only gas station in Upsala, Ontario. The Prairie Embassy Hotel remained six hundred kilometres away. The storm had become worse, which made driving difficult. There were no cars in the lot and no lights on inside the gas station. Aby turned off the engine, pushed back the seat and took off her seat belt. Turning away from her mother, she folded her hands under her head and closed her eyes.

"You're not out of gas again, are you?" said Margaret. These were the first words she'd spoken since Aby had failed to convince her to return to the ocean.

"No," Aby said, not moving. "But we soon will be. This station opens at six."

"Are you sure?"

"Just go to sleep," Aby said, but she did not take her own advice. She listened to the rain hitting the roof of the car. She looked out the window at the other end of the parking lot, where a family of animals was picking through an overflowing garbage can. Aby had never seen these animals before. They had ringed tails and were very focused on their work. They occasionally looked at her with their black-rimmed eyes, in a way that almost seemed like a greeting, although not a friendly one.

Margaret coughed and Aby listened for the rust. It was hard to tell, because the rain was so loud. Aby turned to look at her mother. Margaret's gills were covered by her scarf. She held a white handkerchief to her mouth, which she quickly balled up and tucked into her sleeve. Still looking for evidence, Aby was surprised when her mother spoke.

"Aby, I do owe you an explanation about why I left when I did, without waiting until you were older," Margaret said softly. "I know I should have waited, but I couldn't. I'm sorry I can't give you the whole story. But I can tell you this: I can tell you that there once was a woman who loved two brothers, one a carpenter and the other a tailor. She loved each of them passionately and equally. She would spend the day with the carpenter, and then at night, while he slept, she would walk across the ocean and spend the night with the tailor. Just as the sun rose, she would walk back across the ocean to the carpenter.

"This went on for some time, until one day the carpenter could no longer stand not knowing where she was always going. On the same day, the tailor could no longer stand not knowing where she was always coming from. The carpenter came out to find her as the tailor followed her, and in the middle of the ocean they met.

"Upon seeing each other, the brothers became consumed with jealousy. Each took hold of one of the woman's hands and began trying to pull her back to his side of the ocean. She was literally being torn apart by the jealousy of the two brothers. This went on for three days, until the moon looked down and saw the woman. The moon took pity on the woman and turned her into a shell. The shell slipped from the hands of the brothers and fell beneath the surface of the water.

"Both brothers were overcome with sorrow. For the first time, they truly were brothers, sharing the same grief. They embraced, then heads bowed, each walked back to his side of the ocean. And now the tailor spends the night lifting up his side of the ocean, searching for the shell, while the carpenter sleeps. And when the sun rises, the carpenter lifts up his side of the ocean to search for the shell, while the tailor sleeps. This is what makes the tides."

Aby reached out her hand, which her mother took.

"So you see, the tides are important. It's good that we have the tides," Margaret said.

Both women bowed their heads, letting their stringy hair cover their faces so neither could see that the other was crying. They sat in silence until Margaret pushed out a large breath through her gills and Aby lay back in the driver's seat.

"*Vatn auk tími*?" Margaret asked.

"*Vatn auk tími*," Aby repeated.

Margaret felt a weight leave her—one much larger than she'd anticipated. Her *bjarturvatn* was complete.

There was only one more thing that had to happen, but it was perhaps the most important thing of all. Pushing her hair out of her face, she turned towards her daughter to speak, but Aby spoke first.

"Was it Mr. Honsjtosan?"

"Oh, Aby. Why would you go and ruin it like that?"

"Mr. Dfjal?"

"Certainly not."

"Dr. Bdlks?"

"No."

"That guy, you know … Dad's friend with the loft?"

"That's enough, Aby. That's enough."

Still holding her mother's hand, Aby nodded.

42

The very last one last thing

Sitting inside the cabin, Stewart held a blue HB pencil and stared at the pages of a spiral-bound notebook. The only thing he had to do before his boat was finished was name it. But the task was proving harder than crafting the hull, or even installing the mast. He'd spent almost three years writing down names in the notebook in front of him. Every time Stewart wrote one down, he was sure it was perfect. But some time later, maybe seconds, maybe weeks, Stewart would stroke a line through it.

He wanted the name to be proud and strong, but not arrogant or bullish. It had to be caring, suggesting compassion and empathy, while still confident and firm. It would be a single word, or a phrase so common it had become like a single word.

But even now, when finding the right name was the only task remaining, he still couldn't find it.

The *Good Heart*, he wrote, then stroked a line through it.

~~The *Open Heart*~~

~~The *Grace*~~

The *Lisa*.

Before he'd even lifted his pencil, Stewart knew it was right. He hurried up to the deck. The rain was coming down hard, but Stewart couldn't wait. For the first time in years, he had the sense that his actions were important and that there was no time to lose. Quickly fastening a plastic tarp over the end of the boat, he dried the stern. Using black paint and a flowing, Edwardian script, he delicately painted Lisa on the stern. This simple task gave him great satisfaction.

As he took a step back to look at his work, the Red River spilled its banks and Stewart's feet were covered in water.

43

Something to do

At 8:00 a.m., Rebecca was woken by the ringing of her cellphone. She'd slept well, dreamless and deep. The sound of her phone pleased her, because it gave her something to do. As she'd fallen asleep, Rebecca had felt some apprehension at the prospect of waking up, knowing that she'd have to decide what to do with her day. But for now it was clear: she would answer her cellphone.

Sitting up, Rebecca was disappointed when she saw her phone on her bedside table. It would have been much better if she'd had to search for it. This would have given her another task to accomplish. Without checking the caller I.D., she opened it.

"This is Rebecca Reynolds," she said.

"Rebecca?"

"Who is this?"

"It's Stewart."

"Stewart Findley?"

"How many Stewarts do you know?"

"Three."

"Don't be a smartass."

"I'm not trying to be a smartass."

"You sound really weird."

"But I actually feel really, really good."

"Are you alright?"

"I think I've become, um, emotionally invulnerable."

"You're scaring me."

"But really, I am."

"Look, don't do this to me right now. I'm in the middle of the worst storm I've ever seen. It's unbelievable. I'm in the boat. And it's so weird, because I just finished it and now this. There's a flood. The ground floor of the hotel is already flooding."

"It's raining here too."

"Are you sure you're okay?"

"I think it makes me a little distant."

"What does?"

"Being emotionally invulnerable."

"What's going on with you?"

"I was told that it wouldn't be a good thing, but it feels pretty good. I'm having a lot of problems making decisions, though."

"Okay. This has happened before, no? Remember?"

"I know what you're talking about, but this isn't like that at all. This is different."

"Still, maybe you just need to get out for a bit? You know, get out of the house? Clear your head?"

"I will."

"Wait, wait, wait," Stewart said. "I called to tell you

that I finally named the boat. I've finished the boat. I named her the *Lisa*."

"Okay."

"In honour of your sister."

"That's really nice," Rebecca said. She said this only because she knew it was expected. The information did not cause her to feel anything significant.

She closed her phone, dressed in the same clothes she'd worn yesterday and the day before and left. She did not put on a raincoat, take an umbrella or close the front door behind her.

44

Late checkout

Just after 4:00 p.m., Kenneth entered room #201 at the Prairie Embassy Hotel without knocking. His son was surprised. Rain hit the east-facing window at a right angle, each drop striking as if three more were waiting impatiently behind it. The overhead light was on, but the room remained dark, which made the frequent lightning strikes seem all the more brilliant.

Kenneth stood in the doorway. He had never seen a storm this powerful in his life. "Are you sure you don't know any way to stop it?" he asked his son, shouting to be heard over the sound of the rain.

"I have no idea."

"Then we'd better pack."

"Agreed."

In ten minutes they stood, suitcases in hand, in the front lobby, where the water came up to just below their knees.

"Should we pay?" Anderson asked.

Kenneth stomped his foot in the water, splashing it.

He looked out the window and saw how trees that had been far from the river were now part of it.

"There's no need," he said. "It won't be a hotel for much longer."

They opened the front door of the Prairie Embassy Hotel and stood outside. The rain hurt their faces. Leaving the door open, they waded towards their vehicles. Stopping briefly, they looked up. The storm cloud hovered directly over the hotel, rain pouring out of it. They could see that every cloud, all the way to the horizon, was being pulled towards them. Even as they stood still, staring, already drenched to the bone, the cloud grew larger.

"We'll take my truck, but you drive," Kenneth said to his son. On his way to the passenger door, he stopped. The water had already reached the top of the wheel wells. There was little chance they could drive away. Turning, he looked back at the Prairie Embassy Hotel and saw the sailboat behind it. To his surprise, it no longer looked unfinished. It now had sails. "But that," he said, pointing, "would work much better."

"We did warn them," Anderson replied.

"Agreed."

45

The *Lisa* sails

Stewart was standing on deck, holding the anchor with both hands, when he saw two men wading through the water towards him. As he dropped the anchor overboard, letting go faster than he'd anticipated, he realized that the Lisa had begun to float. Looking back at the two men, Stewart saw that the water was above their knees and rising fast. He found the stepladder and lowered it over the edge to help them board, but the current swirled from the bow and pulled it from his grip.

Stewart watched the water carry the ladder away, surprised that it that it grown so strong, so quickly. Getting down on his stomach, he reached out his arm. The older, taller man grabbed it and pulled himself aboard. The younger one did the same. All three men stood on deck. A bolt of lightning struck a tree near the boat. Only Stewart jumped.

"What should we do with him?" asked Anderson.

"Put him down there."

Anderson grabbed Stewart roughly by the shoulders,

pushing him towards the steps that led down to the cabin.

"Wait! What are you doing?" Stewart protested.

But Anderson was significantly taller and broader, and Stewart couldn't resist. Pushed down the stairs, he landed at the bottom of his boat. He raced back up the steps, but the hatch closed in his face. He heard the lock slip into place.

"What are you doing?" he yelled again. There was no response.

Turning in the small space, Stewart opened the starboard porthole and looked out just in time to see the anchor pulled from the water. He felt the boat begin to move and watched as the Prairie Embassy Hotel got smaller and smaller. It was then that Stewart felt his feet getting wet. Looking down, he saw that water had begun to seep in from the bow.

"Damn it," Stewart said, in a quiet, defeatist tone.

46

The breath of God

Lewis had no idea what time it was when he started to suspect that he was not alone in the suite. He became convinced that someone was standing at the foot of the bed, watching him. He pressed his back against the headboard, wrapped his arms around his legs and suddenly knew, without a doubt, that the intruder was Lisa—the woman he was now convinced was God.

"Get *out* of here!" he said. "I have nothing you want."

Lewis lunged across the bed and punched the air with his fists. When his punches failed to connect, Lewis rolled out of bed and put his arms out in front of him as he walked towards the bathroom. He stopped suddenly and began swinging his fists in all directions. None of these punches struck anything, but the force of his momentum disoriented him, and Lewis became lost in the bedroom.

Raising his arms, Lewis took baby steps until he located the bed. He pressed his back against the headboard and curled his legs against his chest again, but he couldn't convince himself that he was safe. He felt Her breath several times on his cheek. Each time he felt it, Lewis swung with his fists.

"I goddamn know you're here!" he screamed. "Stop watching me!"

47

With the grace water wishes it had

Although the Prairie Embassy Hotel was finally within sight, they were still quite far away when the main road began to flood. Aby looked at her mother. Margaret nodded, and Aby pushed down the right pedal. The car gathered speed. Margaret held the door handle tightly. Water pressed against the floorboards as the car hit a pothole and dipped forward. Water splashed over the hood and the engine, and the white Honda Civic stalled.

Aby repeatedly turned the key in the ignition. The engine refused to start. She opened her door. Water flooded in. Getting out, Aby waded through knee-high water. She circled the white Honda Civic and, after three attempts, opened the passenger door.

"Come on," Aby said. "We'll have to swim from here."

Margaret did not respond. Orange rust fell from the edges of her gills and trickled down her collarbone in a steady stream, staining the collar and front of her shirt and pooling in her lap. She was unconscious.

"No, Mom. Not yet," Aby said.

48

The evaporation of Rebecca Reynolds

Rebecca's wet hair stuck to the side of her face, and the fabric of her shirt clung to her chest in a way that would normally have made her embarrassed. After walking for an indeterminate time, she decided to sit on a bench. This was the first decision she'd made on her own since Zimmer had dropped her off at her apartment the day before, and she felt good about it. Then she doubted herself and thought maybe she should keep walking, but she concluded that she could do this. After several more minutes and much more rain, her cellphone rang.

"Rebecca?"

"Yes."

"They've stolen the boat. They locked me in the cabin. You have to help me."

"Who is this?"

"Stewart!"

"Findley?"

"Just listen to me—"

"I know you. We were very important to each other

for a very long time. You're the most important person in my life, but I work very hard for you to never know that."

"Rebecca, are you on medication again?"

"Why would I do that to you?"

"What's going on?"

"I'm losing myself," Rebecca said. As she said these words, she knew they were true.

"It's going to be okay," Stewart said. Knowing there was little she could do for him, Stewart focused on helping her. "Where are you?"

"I'm sitting on a bench in the park. I don't know the name of it."

"Where is it?"

"It's the one by the art gallery. Behind the art gallery."

"Just stay there. Don't move. Just stay there."

"I don't seem capable of moving now."

"Just stay right there. I'm going to send help."

"Stewart, do you love me?"

"You'll be okay."

"But do you? You don't have to say yes."

"I do. Yes. Still."

"Oh."

"Is that a bad thing?"

"I don't think so," Rebecca said. "I was just hoping that knowing the answer would make me feel something."

Rebecca closed her phone. She sat on the bench. The rain fell harder. She knew the rain couldn't hurt her. She felt impervious to decay. She felt the rain on her skin, but then, all of a sudden, she didn't. When she looked at her arm, she saw that the rain was no longer hitting it but was passing right through. She was, quite literally, beginning to disappear.

49

A triumphant lack of separation

Although Lewis did not know it, it was just before 8:00 p.m. when he put his feet on the carpet, stood, and with only a vague understanding of his motives walked across the room. Although he was sure She was still in the room, he no longer felt She was a threat. If She was going to do something, he figured, She would have done it by now. When his fingers touched the wall, he stretched out his right hand and shuffled along until he felt the windowsill. Standing in front of the window, Lewis was unable to remember how, or if, it opened. He ran his fingers along the frame and found a lock on the sash at the bottom. Lewis unlocked the window and pushed it open. He put his head through and was taken completely off guard by both the rain and the intensity with which it hit his head.

After so many hours without colours or shapes, without music or the human voice, with his world limited to the fabric of the comforter and the edges of the king-sized bed, the feeling of rain on his skin was overwhelming. Lewis rolled up his sleeves. Pulling his head back inside, he took off his shirt and let it fall to the floor, then stood on his tiptoes, extending his naked torso out the window with the sill just below his belly button. Lewis let the rain hit his back and neck and head. He turned so the rain could hit his chest and face, and he was overwhelmed by the thought that the barrier of his skin was irrelevant. Nothing enclosed within it—his heart, his bones, his grief—was separate from anything outside of it. There were no insides and outsides. There were no parts. There was only everything. So far, his only contributions to everything were self-pity, an exaggerated sense of self-importance and one admittedly catchy pop song.

By the time Lewis pulled his head back inside, he knew exactly what he needed to do. First, he shut the window. He felt the soggy carpet between his toes as he extended his arms and took confident strides towards the bathroom. He got dressed, hoping his clothes matched and were clean. He ran his fingers through his wet hair and patted it flat. He had no idea whether he was presentable, but he had done what he could. He followed the wall out of the bathroom and into the living room. Although he knocked the phone to the floor on his first attempt to use it, Lewis managed to pick it up and push the middle button in the bottom row. He counted to fifteen, then requested both assistance and a taxi.

50

Margaret's final request

Aby undid Margaret's seat belt and, cupping water with her hands, washed the rust from her mother's face. She lifted Margaret over her shoulder and began wading towards the Prairie Embassy Hotel. The closer Aby got to the hotel, the higher the water became. At the bottom of the laneway, the water was up to her chest. The front doors were already open, and in the lobby she had to swim, holding her mother in front of her. An end table floated past on a forty-five-degree angle. Books and papers bobbed. Aby carried her mother up the stairs to the second floor.

The door of room #201 was open. Aby laid her mother on the bed. Margaret's breathing was shallow. She coughed and orange syrup spattered out of her gills. Aby left the room and looked down over the banister at the water rising quickly against the walls. Returning to the room and looking out its east-facing window, she saw only water and the tops of trees.

Margaret stirred and Aby returned to the bed.

Margaret opened her eyes and coughed, rust pouring from her gills. "I want a dry death," Margaret said.

"No, Mom. Just try to be still."

"Aby, do you believe in the *trú* ?"

"I'm supposed to be convincing you."

"In my heart I know I'm following my *trú*."

"I know you believe that."

"Then it's simple, Aby. Either you're mistaken about me, or I'm mistaken about my *trú*."

Margaret's eyes closed again. Aby checked her pulse. It was weak. Water began seeping under the door of room #201.

"I'm so sorry," Aby said. She lifted her mother off the bed and set her on the floor. Water trickled under the door and curled under Margaret's head. It rose steadily higher, lifting her hair and spilling onto her face. Aby watched as Margaret's submerged gills opened and she breathed in water.

51

God's audience

Sitting on the edge of the couch in the living room, Lewis
folded his hands together and waited. His hair was still
wet. It did not seem like much time passed before he
felt a gentle tug at his elbow. "Thank you," Lewis said,
standing up.

The hand on his arm felt large and strong. It could
not be Beth, nor could it be Lisa. The hand guided him
out of his room, down the elevator and out of the hotel.
Lewis felt wind on his face. The wind was strong, but
he must have been under an umbrella because he could
feel only an occasional drop of rain on his face. He let
himself be guided down a series of steps, then a second
hand took his other elbow.

"Thank you," Lewis said in the direction of the first.
He let this new hand guide him inside a car, which he
presumed was a taxi. "Please take me to a movie theatre,"
Lewis said. "The closest one."

The taxi moved forward. They made left turns and
right turns. Lewis could smell the remnants of a cigarette

smoked long ago. Feeling that he'd travelled very far from the hotel, he started to feel scared. He couldn't be sure where he was being taken. Reaching out his left hand, Lewis touched the window and ran his hand down the door until he found the handle. He did not open the door, but he kept a firm grip on the handle. Then the car slowed and stopped, and he felt wind on his pants legs from the other direction.

Feeling a tug on his elbow, Lewis slid out of the taxi. He felt rain on his face and hands. The rain was coming down hard, and his clothes quickly became wet. He tripped on the curb, but the driver had his elbow and kept him upright. They walked slowly down a series of steps. He knew they were inside the theatre, because the wind and rain had stopped, and he could smell popcorn.

"Thank you," Lewis said, raising his wallet. The wallet was taken from his hand. Seconds later, he felt it pushed back into his back pocket. Another hand was at his elbow. This one felt feminine.

"I'd like to see the most popular movie you're presenting," Lewis said, and once again held his wallet in the air. With the woman's hand on his elbow, they walked down a gradual slope. Then the hand gently pushed him down. Lewis felt the plush seat underneath him. "Thank you," he said. The hand squeezed his shoulder.

Lewis did not know what movie was playing in front of him or at what point he'd come in. He could not be certain that a movie was playing at all, or if there was anyone in the theatre with him. He sat in his chair, uncomfortable because his pants and jacket were wet from the rain. Then, after what felt like a much longer stretch of time than a standard movie would take, Lewis heard something. It was not music, and it was not dialogue. Lewis did not hear the movie at all. The small sound he heard was the audience.

The events on the screen had scared the audience, which made them quiet. Lewis understood that the audience was afraid, and he became afraid too. The next time the audience was quiet, Lewis could tell it was because they were sad, and so he became sad. He heard when they were anxious or upset or hopeful, and he became these things as well.

Soon he could hear the movie—the music and the soundtrack and the dialogue—but Lewis continued to listen only to the audience, reacting as they did. Near the end of the film, when the boy had successfully won the girl and the audience was relieved because everything was going to be okay, Lewis looked down and noticed that his shirt was inside out.

52

The roof of the Prairie Embassy Hotel

Aby watched her mother breathe underneath the water. Margaret's breaths were very deep and very far apart.

Aby had spent years trying to predict what her mother would look like when she saw her again. Innumerable times she'd taken childhood memories and aged them, greying her mother's hair and deepening her wrinkles. But the face she saw in front of her looked little like the one she'd created in her mind. Her mother had aged in ways that Aby could never have predicted, shaped not just by time but also by her unwatered life.

Slipping beneath the surface, Aby put her head next to her mother's. She breathed in and out, then slowed her breath until their gills were in sync. She felt a deep sadness as she allowed herself to accept that the mother she remembered, the mother she had come to rescue, didn't exist and perhaps never had. Aby wrapped her arms around Margaret and swam into the hallway.

Using the railing for support, Aby half swam, half climbed the steps to the fifth floor. Her progress was slow.

The water rose almost as fast as she climbed and it was to her waist when she opened the door to room #501. She opened the room's only window. With her mother over her shoulder, she climbed out onto the roof.

She put her mother down. Margaret coughed as she took in air again. Dead birds and car batteries were scattered across the roof. Aby looked around her; as far as she could see, there was nothing but water. Even now, water was lapping at her feet. Quickly, Aby lifted her mother in her arms. The water rose to her waist, and Aby lifted Margaret over her head. The cloud above her seemed low enough to touch. The water rose to Aby's shoulders, then up her neck and over her face. Aby held her mother as high as she could. Her arms and legs ached. The rain fell. She felt the water reach her forearms. She felt her mother's body tighten and then go limp.

Aby looked up, through the water, and saw a blinding flash of blue light. She did not resist as the current lifted Margaret's body out of her grip and carried her away.

53

A beacon, sudden and timely

Anderson and Kenneth stood on deck, watching the rain strike the water. The wind was loud and the sound of thunder almost constant, and when Anderson spoke he used a voice so hushed and small that his father had to lean towards him to hear it.

"We couldn't have known," Anderson said. "How could we have known?"

Anderson looked at his father, who looked out at the storm. Then they looked at each other. For a moment the thunder stopped, the wind died down, and the only sound they could hear was Stewart banging on the hatch.

"How many people do you think would fit on this boat?" Kenneth asked.

"Quite a few, I bet."

No verbal or physical cue followed, but a decision was made and passed between them. Anderson unlocked the hatch, Kenneth opened it, and Stewart charged up the steps, his hands in fists. But when he reached the deck, he was brought to a halt by the view around him. Lowering his arms, he turned in a circle. In every direction, all the way to the horizon, there was nothing but water.

"We want to use your boat to help."

"Help who?" Stewart said, gesturing at the water that surrounded them.

"Well, Winnipeg's pretty close, right?"

Stewart looked up at the small Canadian flag attached to the top of the mast. He watched it flap in the steadily increasing wind. For the first time in years, and certainly since he'd taken employment at the Prairie Embassy Hotel, Stewart felt a sense of purpose. Finally, there was something he *must*—not just could—accomplish. He began moving quickly, his motions decisive, giving him an unquestionable authority.

"You, the thin one," Stewart said.

"Anderson."

"Anderson, take the rudder and keep us pointed into the wind. And you . . ."

"Kenneth."

"Remove the halyard ... unfasten that thing," Stewart said, pointing.

All three men began working quickly and collectively. The halyard was attached to the headboard. The mainsail was allowed to run free. But as Stewart was raising the sail hand over hand, he suddenly stopped and looked around. He looked over the bow and the stern and the starboard side, but there was no point of reference. They had no map. No compass. No way to determine what direction to sail in.

"Which way?" Stewart asked.

Just then, a blinding blue light flashed in the distance.

None of the men knew that the blue light had anything to do with Margaret, or that it was above the roof of the Prairie Embassy Hotel, which was now completely underwater. Nor did they know that sailing directly towards it would set them on a straight-line course to Winnipeg. But all three felt that the blue light's sudden and timely appearance was unlikely to be a coincidence.

"I presume we're going that way?" Anderson asked.

"Definitely," Stewart replied. "And you, Kenneth, get down in the cabin, start bailing and keep at it."

54

The last full-sized telephone booth in the world

Lewis left the movie theatre and began searching for a telephone. All the stores were closed. No cars stopped; they just splashed water on him as they passed. He did not know where his cellphone was—the last time he remembered using it was back in Toronto, which seemed like a very long time ago. The puddles were now so large, and his clothes were already so drenched, that he stopped avoiding puddles and simply walked through them.

At the corner of Albert and McDermot, Lewis found what he assumed was the last full-sized phone booth in the world. Closing the door behind him, Lewis wiped the rain off his face with the sleeve of his jacket. He shook his head, sending beads of water onto the Plexiglas. After so long without colours and sounds, even the black of the plastic receiver and the rain against the Plexiglas were overwhelming.

Lewis had to close his eyes to remember the number his wife had forced him to memorize. The phone began to ring. After the third ring, a click indicated that the call had been answered, but no one spoke.

"Rebecca? Are you there?"

"Yes, I am."

"I don't have much time, so please listen."

"Who is this?"

"It's Lewis. Just listen."

"Lewis Taylor?"

"Rebecca, you were right. So right. I treated your sister badly. I never noticed that she was my whole life. Forgive me that I only learned this after she died."

Lewis waited for a response, but none came. The phone went dead. Looking down, he saw that water had pooled at the bottom of the phone booth and was quickly rising.

55

The unanticipated effects
of the unexpected apology

Rain soaked into Rebecca's clothes and Lewis's apology began to dissolve her emotional invulnerability. She looked at her hands. The flesh was solid, and she felt more open and free than she ever had before.

It was a fragile state, Rebecca knew, and to sustain it she began thinking of Stewart. Working chronologically, she pictured each significant moment in their relationship. She saw him kneeling behind the damaged tail light. She watched him tinker with the engine of the Karmann Ghia. She saw him on their first date, the day they moved in together, their wedding day.

Each memory returned to her so clearly that she forgot about the park and the bench and the rain. Each moment she remembered, she almost relived. A tiny residue of her feelings for Stewart had remained inside her: the combination of her new vulnerability with the vividness of the remembered moments created a tiny opening. As she pictured the day Stewart left her, Rebecca began to fall in love with him again.

She tried to pick up her cellphone, but it passed through her fingers. Her state was now so advanced that there was only one thing that could save her, something that part of her—her pride, or her fear, or both—had stopped her from doing before. For three years she'd been unable to make herself do it. And even now, even though she knew that making this call was her only chance, she was still hesitant to do it.

56

The cloud thief

As Aby swam down towards the Prairie Embassy Hotel, she tried to justify what she had seen—it was the rust reacting with something in the air, or a mirage, or a trick of her tired eyes. She could not bring herself to believe the most obvious explanation: the first sign that a *koma upplifa* has passed is a flash of blue light. But Aby knew that once a *koma upplifa* enters a cloud, it absorbs the cloud entirely, using the cloud's strength to travel to the next world. Although there was some debate about how long it took a soul to fuse with a cloud, it was generally believed to be just under two hours.

When Aby reached the hotel, she swam through open doors and out windows, into rooms and back outside. She delighted in her renewed ability to go up when she wanted to and down when she wanted to. She swam up all five flights of stairs, then dove straight down through the middle. She made loop-de-loops in the lobby. When she was sure that at least two hours had gone by, Aby swam back up to the surface.

Hovering just below the water, she kept her eyes closed; she could not bring herself to look. She reached her hand out of the water. She felt no rain on her skin. Opening her eyes, she gave a tiny kick and pushed her head above the surface. The rain had stopped. She did not see lightning or hear thunder. She looked at the sky and saw that the cloud was shrinking.

"Well, I'll be damned," Aby said, although for the first time in her life she knew she wasn't. She dove under the surface and began swimming, although she hadn't yet decided where she would go.

57

A sailboat at Portage and Main

With the wind pushing the sailboat at just under forty knots, Stewart and the rainmakers arrived in Winnipeg in just under two hours. The water continued to rise. They travelled into the city on the Red River, and then began sailing through streets as if they were tributaries.

Stewart stayed at the rudder as they navigated between office towers and through the intersection of Portage and Main. Anderson and Kenneth took turns leaning over the side and plucking survivors from the water. They rescued people clinging to lampposts and temporary rafts made of doors and debris. Survivors jumped from the roofs of buildings to swim up to the boat. There were more than forty people aboard when Anderson spotted a man treading water, his exhaustion evident. When he was pulled over the side of the boat, he began to thank everyone aboard. It was some time before he worked his way to the stern and recognized the man at the rudder.

"Stewart?" Lewis asked, his voice full of disbelief.

"Lewis?" Stewart replied, just as bemused. He wanted

to say how sorry he was about Lisa. He wanted to marvel at this uncanny reunion. But he knew they had no time. "Later. We'll get into it later," he said. "Just get down to the cabin and bail."

Lewis obeyed. He joined the long line of people passing bucket after bucket back and forth. Although they had to keep bailing at a furious pace, the boat did not sink. The people on deck continued plucking survivors from the water. Even when the deck had no more room, more and more people were pulled on board.

Stewart had no idea how much time passed, but just as the rain stopped, his cellphone rang. It was Rebecca's number.

58

Repressing nothing

Rebecca waited for her hand to become firm again, picked up her phone, and then dialled Stewart's number.

"Stewart?" she said. She couldn't place where he was, but a considerable crowd seemed to be very happy about something.

"Rebecca! Hello! It stopped raining. The rain has stopped!"

"I just. I wanted to ask you . . ."

"Speak up! I can hardly hear you."

"This is hard for me."

"That means it's important. So just say it, Rebecca. Just say it out loud."

"I want you to come home," she said.

Stewart did not immediately answer, but through the line she heard many people rejoicing.

"Soon," Stewart said. "I'll be there very, very soon."

The phone no longer felt soft in her hand. In front of her was a man walking his dog. Feeling Rebecca's joy, he turned and stared, but Rebecca did not care. She didn't care that the teenagers on the other side of the park could feel what she was feeling. Or that everyone driving past could feel it. Or that people in their living rooms three blocks away could feel it. Rebecca did not care that anyone and everyone could feel what she felt and she knew that she would never care again.

Acknowledgements

The following people contributed to this book more than they will ever know: Anne, Angelika and Sam. Zach, Suzanne, Ian and the Impostors and Rosemary. Andy and Mary. Chris and Rob. Stephanie, Alana, Rebecca, Michele. Rolly, Shirley, Liz, Karen and Barry, Marlo, Phoenix and Frida.

I'd also like to gratefully acknowledge the financial support of The Canada Council for the Arts, the Ontario Arts Council and Lamport/Sheppard Productions.

Also Available

ANDREW KAUFMAN

ALL MY FRIENDS ARE SUPERHEROES

All Tom's friends really are superheroes. Tom even married a superhero, the Perfectionist. But at their wedding the Perfectionist is hypnotized by her ex, Hypno, to believe that Tom is invisible. Nothing he does can make her see him.

Six months later the Perfectionist is sure that Tom has abandoned her, so she's moving to Vancouver. She'll use her superpowers to leave all the heartbreak behind. With no idea that Tom's beside her, she boards the plane. Tom has until they touch down to convince her he's there, or he loses her forever ...

A wonderful, heartbreakingly funny tribute to love, sweet love.

Praise for ALL MY FRIENDS ARE SUPERHEROES

"An adorable book." *Toby Litt*

"The quirkiest, funniest romance of the year." *Marie Phillips*

"Genius ... I read it on the train home the day I received it and spent the whole evening smiling." *Scott Pack*, menadmybigmouth Blog